Viv glanced at the baby and then at Chase.

"He's getting fussy. Would you mind picking him up and holding him for a minute?"

"Me?" Chase's eyes widened. He went very still.

"Hold him close to you, up against your chest," Viv prompted. "He'll feel more secure that way."

But would Chase feel secure?

He pulled Theo to him. Immediately, the baby dropped his head to Chase's shoulder and heaved a sigh.

Chase felt something stir inside him.

How in the world would he ever make Viv understand that he couldn't be the man she wanted him to be?

Books by Charlotte Carter

Love Inspired

Montana Hearts
Big Sky Reunion
Big Sky Family
Montana Love Letter
Home to Montana
Montana Wrangler
Tail of Two Hearts

CHARLOTTE CARTER

A multipublished author of more than fifty romances, cozy mysteries and inspirational titles, Charlotte Carter lives in Southern California with her husband of forty-nine years and their cat, Mittens. They have two married daughters and five grandchildren. When she's not writing, Charlotte does a little stand-up comedy, "G-Rated Humor for Grown-ups," and teaches workshops on the craft of writing.

Tail of Two Hearts

Charlotte Carter

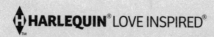

Special thanks and acknowledgment are given
to Charlotte Carter for her contribution to
The Heart of Main Street miniseries.

Recycling programs
for this product may
not exist in your area.

LOVE INSPIRED BOOKS

ISBN-13: 978-0-373-81726-9

TAIL OF TWO HEARTS

Copyright © 2013 by Harlequin Books S.A.

www.Harlequin.com

Printed in U.S.A.

And now these three remain: faith, hope and love.
But the greatest of these is love.
—*1 Corinthians* 13:13

I'd like to thank my fellow authors of the Heart of Main Street continuity series. With such a complicated story with recurring characters and overarching story lines, it takes exceptional communication and cooperation among the authors. Arlene James, Carolyne Aarsen, Brenda Minton, Lissa Manley and Valerie Hansen, you made my work easy. And thanks to Emily Rodmell, our editor, who kept us all going in the right direction.

Thanks to Gina H. and Laura W. from the Harlequin Forums for the lovely Thanksgiving table decorations.

Special thanks to Charlie; you know why.

Chapter One

Vivian Duncan stepped out of Happy Endings Bookstore onto the sidewalk in the small Kansas town of Bygones. Watching leaves and bits of paper racing down the street blown by a brisk breeze, she inhaled the crisp November air. Only a few weeks until Thanksgiving, one of her favorite times of the year.

Her mother made the best turkey and stuffing, and her older siblings who had moved away from home always made it a point to come back for the holiday.

A gaggle of laughing and shouting schoolchildren barreled past her en route to Fluff & Stuff, the pet store that had opened on Main Street in July. Vivian was on her way there as well, just two doors down the street. The colorful awnings above each of the new stores fluttered in the breeze.

She hoped the owner of Fluff & Stuff, Chase

Rollins, would help her put together a special event at the bookstore to promote books about dogs.

Who better to ask for help on the topic than Chase?

As she opened the door, she faced the big green-cheeked parrot near the cash register who squawked his greeting, "What's up? What's up?" He proudly bobbed his head and did a little dance on his perch.

"Hello, Pepper." Vivian smiled at Chase's recently acquired bird that was looking for a new home.

"Good birdie! Good birdie!" he vocalized.

"I'm sure you are." She looked around for Chase. Hearing the high-pitched voices of the youngsters she'd seen running into the shop, she headed toward the back where puppies were kept in a pen.

She eased past two boys who were running Chase's dog, Boyo, through his trick repertoire: rollover, shake, play dead. The ridiculous-looking bassetoodle—a combination of a basset hound and poodle—performed brilliantly for the boys, and they all vied for a chance to show off their skills with the dog.

"It's my turn! It's my turn!" one boy insisted.

"You don't even know what to do," an older youngster complained.

"I do so!"

From a shelf high above the action, Fluff, a long-haired cat with enough hair for two, looked down on the action with disdain. Vivian gave Fluff a scratch between her ears.

"You're too smart to do their bidding, aren't you?" she whispered to the cat.

Fluff responded with a faint purr.

Chase really did love his animals. For that matter, so did Vivian.

She walked past displays of dog and cat beds, stacks of canned and dried animal food, and toys for all manner of pets and finally found him supervising the youngsters around the puppy pen. He made sure they didn't manhandle the puppies too badly but did socialize them to make for better pets.

His warm brown eyes lit up when he spotted Vivian, and he produced a delighted smile. "Hey, Viv. How's Roger doing?"

"He's doing fine—healthy and active." She chuckled at the reference to the hamster she'd purchased from Chase and had named in honor of Roger Bannister, the first man to break the four-minute mile. "He's so busy running on his wheel and playing with his toys. If I want to get any peace and quiet, I have to put him in the extra bedroom."

"They can be pretty active."

Still smiling, he stepped toward Vivian. When she'd first met him, she'd thought he was an attractive man. She still did. At six foot two with a muscular body, he towered over her five foot four, even when she was wearing heels. His short dark hair had a natural wave that sculpted his head. His nose was straight, his lips nicely full. If it weren't for a slight scar on his chin, he might be too handsome. But the scar gave him an air of mystery.

"What can I do for you?" he asked.

"I, uh..." Snapping back from her train of thought, she started over. "Allison and I at Happy Endings have realized books about dogs are particularly popular. We'd like to put on a special event and thought you could give us some guidance about where to get a dog or two for show-and-tell. I know the puppies you have are from the local shelter."

"That's right. The puppies and kittens from Happy Havens Animal Shelter attract customers and sometimes get adopted, so it's a win-win situation."

"Either way, it's a nice thing you're doing." In the short time she'd known Chase, she'd discovered he had a generous heart, particularly when it came to animals.

Chase kept one eye on the boys and the puppies as he spoke. "I like the idea of my customers rescuing a dog and giving it a good home."

"I do, too." Admiration for his principles filled her chest. "I wonder if it would be best to show off the puppies for our event or find some older dogs."

"I'd say older dogs. For one thing, they're much harder to place in a new home, and the shelter is overflowing with them right now. Plus, most of them have at least some training. Trying to explain something when you've got a handful of puppies would be like a juggler trying to give a speech."

She chuckled at the image. "Using older dogs sounds like it would be for the best. If you have the time, we'd like you to be part of the event, talk about breeds, training, care and feeding. That sort of thing. We thought that would bring attention to both businesses."

"Sure. I'd be happy to come talk about dogs." He noticed someone at the cash register, and they both walked in that direction.

"I'm a big supporter of the local shelter," he said. "Since Randall Manufacturing closed down the factory and laid off their employees, the turnover forced a lot of people to surrender their pets. Some of those folks are moving away, and their new places don't allow animals. Or they're broke and can't afford to feed their animals."

"That's a shame." Her family had always had dogs and cats around the wheat farm. She'd hate the thought of handing any of them over to a shelter. Even a no-kill shelter. They were always a part of the family.

He stepped behind the counter to help his customer. "Hello, Mrs. Murdock. How's your arthritis doing these days?"

"Not bad for now, but if it gets cold and rainy, it'll act up. I can be sure of that."

He scanned the sack of cat food Mrs. Murdock had placed on the counter. "Anything else today? We're starting to get in some nice toys and soft beds for Christmas gifts. Your Sadie might like one of those."

She tilted her head. "I do believe you're trying to tempt me, Mr. Rollins."

"Only because I know how much you love to spoil Sadie."

Mrs. Murdock gave Chase a twenty-dollar bill. Chase made change, and Mrs. Murdock went out the door smiling.

"Come again! Come again!" the parrot squawked.

Chase ignored the bird. "The shelter is getting overcrowded, so I've started a monthly Adopt a Pet Day here at the shop. In fact I'm having one this Saturday." He handed her a flyer from the stack on the counter.

"What a nice thing for you to do." She glanced over the flyer, which featured a cute poodle with a pink bow on top of her head. "She sure is a cutie."

"Yeah, she is. The big dogs are the ones they have the most trouble placing in new homes. They need a lot of space and eat a lot of food."

She chuckled. "I'm sure they do. But if you're doing your adoption day, will you be able to leave the pet store to talk to our people?"

"I've got a friend who can fill in for me. It'll be okay."

"I'm glad." She was relieved, too, that Chase could help out.

"When you visit the shelter, you'll have to be careful not to fall in love." His eyes twinkled, and his lively grin was pure temptation.

Vivian blinked. Her cheeks flushed. Had he said *fall in love?* With who? And why had she zeroed in on that thought?

"Some of those dogs are pretty lovable," he continued, unaware of her reaction. "You might want to adopt one or two yourself."

She chided herself for misunderstanding what he meant. "Uh, no, I'll have to stick with Roger and my cat, Essie, for now."

"That's all right." His eyes glinted with humor. "Chances are good I'll have another opportunity to tempt you with a puppy or two. I don't give up easily."

She nodded, thinking that was an admirable trait. "I'm sure that's true. I'll just have to do my very best to resist your persuasive ways."

His brown-eyed gaze softened as he studied her face. "I can only hope you won't try too hard to resist."

She swallowed hard. Chase Rollins was a man who knew how to flirt, and she was reacting just the way he had intended: with a nervous flutter in her stomach.

She stepped toward the door. "I'll tell Allison about the shelter, and that you'll help us out."

"Right. I'll be happy to."

Vivian pulled the door open and escaped outside just as the flame of embarrassment heated her cheeks.

Her recent forays into the dating world had been less than successful. Indeed, they'd been a flop. As soon as she had announced to the men in question that she'd never be able to give them a baby, the guys had dumped her.

She had always dreamed of having a big family. Apparently God had decided two years ago, when she had had her hysterectomy, that she wouldn't be able to give birth to her own children. But that wouldn't prevent her from having the family she wanted. She'd recently taken charge of her dream by putting in her application at several agencies to adopt a baby.

Since the guys she'd dated had been clear about wanting to have children who carried their own genes, she'd decided being a single mother was the way she would go. Even though she knew some people would not approve of her choice, she was determined to set her dream in motion.

She had faith that God understood how she had longed for children and would provide when the time came.

* * *

Chase watched Vivian until she moved out of view toward the bookstore.

"Pretty lady. Pretty lady," Pepper chanted.

"Yes, Pepper, she is pretty. Nice, too." In the few months since Chase had arrived in Bygones and had opened the pet store, he'd enjoyed her visits to the shop. He liked seeing her walk in the door with her auburn hair swinging at her shoulders. An eager smile on her face and a smattering of cute freckles across her nose. A bounce in her step.

She liked animals, too. Vivian gave Boyo a pat or Fluff a chuck under the chin as she strolled through the shop.

And she was smart. Until the town of Bygones had come on hard times, she'd been a librarian. Which meant she sure had a lot more education than he did. He hadn't dropped out of high school, but working a night shift at a warehouse in Wichita during his senior year had made his grades tank. He'd been grateful to graduate.

He'd worked at the warehouse for nearly thirteen years until he had moved to Bygones for the chance to open a business of his own.

Strolling to the back of the store, he joined the boys around the puppy pen. "Puppies need a lot of sleep, kids. Why don't you let these guys rest now? You can come back tomorrow." *And bring your moms and dads along so you can talk them into adopting one of these lovable guys,* he added silently. "Tell your folks we've got some cute puppies down here."

"I already have, Mr. Rollins," one little boy with a missing front tooth piped up. "My mom said she didn't want to clean up after a puppy."

Chase bent down to the boy's level and looked him in the eye. "You can tell your mom that the animal shelter has dogs who need a home and are already housebroken."

"Really?" The boy's eyes brightened.

"Absolutely."

"Come on, Becker." He tugged on a younger boy's jacket. "We gotta get home 'n tell Mom."

The twosome plus the rest of the puppy lovers raced for the door.

Chase smiled to himself. Maybe there'd be one fewer dog looking for a home at Happy Havens Animal Shelter by the weekend.

He'd like that. A lot.

And the chance to see Viv again.

When Vivian returned to the bookstore, Allison was helping Oliver Fibley, a regular customer, search on the computer for a new book about stamp collecting. Knowing he was such a devoted philatelist, Vivian imagined he already owned every book ever printed on the subject.

"Hello, Mr. Fibley." Her cheerful greeting caused him to lift his gaze from the computer screen.

In his usual sweet way, he nodded and gave her a small smile.

Vivian was anxious to tell Allison about Chase's idea to use shelter dogs for their event, but she could wait until Mr. Fibley left. For now she'd keep herself busy by reshelving the books in the Kids' Korner section, where children's books were located. Just as it had been when she had worked in the library, she found young readers often didn't return books to their proper place.

She adjusted her casual calf-length skirt so she wouldn't step on the hem and squatted down to re-order the books.

A few minutes later, after seeing Mr. Fibley out, Allison joined Vivian in the children's section. She sat down on one of the child-size chairs. Her pink T-shirt was stenciled with the slogan "No act of kindness, no matter how small, is ever wasted. Aesop."

"So what did Chase think of our idea for Doggie Daze?" she asked.

Crouched down in front of the lowest bookshelf, Vivian smiled at the name her boss had given their event. "He thought it was a great idea. He suggested we borrow a couple of dogs from the shelter."

"I hadn't thought about that." Surprise raised Allison's nicely arched brows. "I was just thinking that he always has puppies in his shop. The kids go crazy for them."

"True. But Chase thinks the event will go better with older dogs who have some training."

"Good point. Then that's what we'll do."

"Sounds good to me." Vivian shifted aside the books on the lowest shelf and slipped one into place.

"Viv? You're smiling."

"I smile most of the time, don't I?"

Allison eyed her curiously. "Of course you do. But it's a different kind of smile. Did something happen at the pet shop?"

"Not really." She sat on her heels. "It's just that…"

"That what?" Allison pressed.

"I think Chase was flirting with me. But it was probably my imagination."

"It was not your imagination. You're a very attractive woman, and he's a very nice man. And he's single. He'd have to be blind not to notice you and be interested."

"Maybe." Vivian pushed to her feet. "He doesn't know I'm hoping to adopt a baby. When he finds out, he'll probably lose interest in me in a hurry."

Allison's jaw dropped. "Why on earth would he do that?"

"Because in the past year, two guys I had been dating dropped me like an overdue book when I told them I couldn't have children of my own." The memory still had the power to sting and made her uneasy about mentioning to anyone her inability to reproduce.

"Oh, honey." Standing, Allison rested her hand on Vivian's shoulder and gave her a squeeze. "Chase may not be like that. You can't think that all men are like the two who dumped you. If he's interested, you need to give him a chance."

"It doesn't seem right to keep something like that a secret."

"Well, yes, I suppose that's true. But just because he flirted a little doesn't mean you have to blurt it out right away or tell him you've applied to adopt a baby. You may find you don't even like him."

If her reaction this morning was any sign, Vivian was pretty sure she'd like him a lot. She certainly felt a spark.

"If Chase is the right man for you," Allison continued, "he might be surprised about you adopting on your own. I know I was when you first told me. But I soon realized how much you want a family, and I'm all for it. The sooner, the better, right? I mean, I get to be Auntie Alli, don't I?"

Laughing at Allison's sweet request, Vivian felt some of the tension leave her. "Absolutely!"

"Good." Allison glanced at her shiny new engagement ring and twisted it around her finger. "Meanwhile I get to work on being the best stepmother ever to Sam's twins."

"I'm sure Rosie and Nicky already love you."

Vivian felt a twinge of envy. There had been a rash of engagements going on in Bygones lately. Just last Friday, Lily Farnsworth, who owned the flower shop next door to the bookstore, had married Tate Bronson, a local farmer and single dad. And now Allison was happily making plans for her wedding to the high school basketball coach.

"I certainly hope they love me. I already adore them." Allison patted Vivian's shoulder again. "I'll leave it to you to talk with the folks at the animal shelter. We're going to need to put together a flyer about Doggie Daze to post around town and get an announcement in the *Gazette*."

"Maybe we can even get Whitney to write a story about it. That would be good publicity." Whitney, the newspaper's one reporter, was always looking for some local angle.

"It would indeed. I'll give her a call. And since you are way better at graphics than I am, I'll let you design the flyer."

"I'd love to. My inner artist enjoys being let loose from time to time."

Between assisting customers and designing the Doggie Daze flyer, Viv saw the rest of the day go by quickly.

After Allison decided to close for the day, Vivian grabbed her purse and jacket from the back room, and stepped outside to head home.

It was well into twilight; the old-fashioned wrought-iron streetlights were lit, casting circles of yellow on the brick street that ran through downtown. Wrought-iron benches spaced periodically along the sidewalk stood empty and only a few parked cars remained.

As she strolled to her car, she noticed the shop lights were off at Fluff & Stuff. In the upstairs apartment where Chase lived, a shadow crossed a lit but curtained window. Chase was such a nice, down-to-earth guy; he seemed almost too good to be true.

But she'd been burned twice and was leery about how he might react when she had to tell him about her inability to have babies. *If* they got that far.

Exhaling, she climbed into her compact car for the short ride home. No sense worrying about that now, she told herself.

Because her parents lived thirty minutes from Bygones, Vivian had rented a small house closer to her job at the library when she had first started to work there. But then the town had run out of money, had cut the funds for her position and had reduced the number of hours the library was open.

Vivian had been fortunate to be hired by Allison to help at the bookstore.

Her house formerly belonged to a foreman on the now-bankrupt wheat farm. The two-bedroom clapboard house served her well. And the rent was modest enough that she could still afford it, even though she was only working part-time at Happy Endings.

She stopped on the road in front of her mailbox and grabbed the day's mail, then drove under the carport.

Taking her mail and purse, she went in the front door and flicked on the light.

Essie, her calico cat, hopped down from her favorite spot on the back of the couch, tiptoeing over to meet Vivian.

"Hi there, little lady." She crouched down to pet the cat. "Have you had a busy day watching out the window?"

Essie responded with a loud, rumbling purr.

"Yes, it sounds like it was very exciting." Vivian tossed her purse and mail on the blond-wood end table by the couch. Although she had purchased mostly used furnishings, she'd perked up the room with two bright red garden stools for coffee tables and a couple of matching red throw pillows, accented with a green-and-white afghan her mother had crocheted tossed over the back of the couch. On the longest wall, she had hung framed posters of colorful gardens from around the world.

Definitely homier than plain walls and a beige couch.

She stepped into the second bedroom, where

Roger was noisily running through his tunnel, showing off his speed.

"Hi, guy. Did you get in lots of training today?" She peered into his cage, which sat on top of an old wooden desk. "Chase asked about you this morning."

Roger peeked out of his tunnel and gazed up at her with his beady little eyes.

"I know. He really loves animals—even little guys like you."

As she glanced around the small bedroom, she pictured a crib and changing table, maybe a mural of Noah's ark on the wall.

Just because she couldn't bear her own children didn't mean she couldn't have a family. She didn't need a man to tell her it was okay to fulfill her dream. She was taking charge of her own life.

Essie wound her way between Vivian's legs, still purring loudly.

"I know, sweetie. You want some dinner, don't you?"

In the kitchen, Vivian poured some dry food into the cat dish, placed it on the floor for Essie and returned to the living room. Plopping down on the couch, she kicked off her shoes and picked up the mail.

An ad for a pizza place on Highway 135. A solicitation from some charity she'd never heard of. And a—

The envelope—bearing the return address of one of several adoption agencies she had contacted about adopting a baby—trembled in her hand.

She swallowed hard and licked her lips.

Please, please let it be good news.

Carefully she opened the envelope and removed the single sheet of stationery.

Dear Miss Duncan, Vivian read. *We appreciate your interest in adopting a child from our agency. However—*

Her eyes began to blur the words: *single woman... limited income...not financially equipped to support a child.*

She covered her mouth with her hand. *It's only one agency turning me down,* she told herself. She'd applied to several others. Somewhere there was a baby waiting for a mommy. Waiting for *her* to hold and love him.

She straightened her shoulders.

Tomorrow was another day. She was confident her dream would come true. She swallowed her tears and lifted her chin.

All in God's time.

Chapter Two

As was his custom, Chase woke early the next morning. He let Boyo out the back door to a fenced area where he could do his business. The dog sniffed the perimeter of his domain. Boyo relaxed only after he was convinced that there had been no intruders since his last visit.

Before long Boyo was back in the shop and racing up the stairs for his breakfast. His brownish coat was a typical shade for a basset hound but his curly hair was very much that of a poodle.

Chase trotted up the stairs behind him.

The fact that he owned a pet shop still amazed him. His life had definitely turned around the day some anonymous benefactor had decided to revitalize downtown Bygones and had offered matching funds for six new businesses to start up in the refurbished stores on Main Street.

The minute he'd heard about the opportunity,

he'd sent in his application. Until then, owning a pet store had only been a fanciful dream born of a few happy months as a youngster volunteering at an animal shelter outside of Wichita, plus a whole menagerie of strays he'd brought home over the years.

By the time he was a teenager, his reality had been working grueling, mostly boring, hours, first as a worker and then as foreman, in a warehouse near Wichita.

He had hated the drudgery of the job; he had ever since starting to work there as a teenager. But the wages had been enough that his mother had been able to cut back on the hours she had worked.

In the small upstairs kitchen he fixed Boyo and Fluff their breakfasts. While they ate, he stood at the counter eating a bowl of cereal and drinking his morning coffee.

As soon as he fed the puppies and kittens downstairs, and cleaned their pens, he would keep his eye out for Vivian's car. He'd been thinking about her a lot. Eager to see her again. Although he wasn't sure that was a good idea, he couldn't seem to help himself.

An hour later, just as he was finishing with Pepper's cage, Chase spotted Vivian's little red car go by.

"What's up? What's up?" Pepper squawked.

"I'm going to call on a very pretty lady. That's what's up."

"Pretty birdie. Pretty birdie," Pepper announced in his shrill vocalization.

"Yes, Pepper, I know." Chase held out his hand so Pepper could hop off his shoulder, onto his hand and return to his clean cage with fresh newspapers on the bottom. A fine use for the local *Bygones Gazette,* he was sure.

The parrot reached his perch and gave his feathers a shake. "Good birdie. Good birdie."

"You're an excellent birdie, Pepper. I'm hoping one day soon you'll find a new home." Although he had to admit he was growing fond of the silly bird, he'd be more than happy to sell Pepper to a parrot lover. Business was business, right?

The middle-aged man who had brought in the bird had told Chase that Pepper had belonged to his mother, now deceased. His wife hated the bird. So he had to get rid of Pepper.

It was hard on long-lived creatures like large parrots. When their owner passed on, the birds experienced grief much like humans did. But after a few weeks here in the pet store, Pepper seemed to be adjusting to his temporary home and clearly enjoyed greeting customers.

Sometimes not too politely, Chase thought with a frown.

"I'll find you a permanent home soon, ol' codger," he promised. Unfortunately he hadn't had a single response to his advertisement so far.

Chase washed his hands and tried to tame the lock of hair that kept falling down over his forehead, to no avail.

Outside, another sunny but cool morning greeted him. The school day had already started, and none of the shops had opened yet, so there was little traffic on the street.

Despite the Closed sign on Happy Endings's door, Chase knocked on the glass window. He peered inside until he saw movement in the shop. Then he stepped back and cleared his throat. Absently, he rubbed his damp palms on his pants and shuffled his feet. She wasn't expecting to see him today, and he wasn't sure how she'd react to his idea for Saturday.

Vivian lifted the sign and saw him. Her pretty blue eyes widened, and he heard her unlock the door. Her expression was both surprised and wary as she greeted him.

"Sorry to come by so early, but I wanted to talk with you," Chase said.

"Sure." She opened the door wider. "Is it about our Doggie Daze event?"

"Yeah, sort of." He stepped inside. As she closed the door behind him, Chase caught the fresh scent of citrus—Viv's perfume or shampoo, he suspected. It mixed pleasantly with the unique smell of books and printer's ink. He glanced around the shop— the walls painted in blue, green and tan—and its dozens of bookcases with their shelves filled with books. He noted that Allison apparently hadn't arrived for work yet.

"I wondered if you'd like to go with me to the Happy Havens shelter tomorrow?" he asked. "You could check out the dogs, decide which ones you'd like to bring in for your Doggie Daze affair."

"I'd love to! I'm sure Allison would let me come in a little late. She's very excited about the event."

Her eager response, and the way her eyes crinkled at the corners when she smiled, delighted Chase. He was already looking forward to spending a little time with Viv. Getting to know her better. Just as friends, he reminded himself. He wasn't looking for a romantic relationship. He had broken up with a woman in Wichita only a few months ago. No need to get involved again too quickly.

They made plans to meet at his shop in the morning, and he'd drive them to the shelter.

"Say, I put on a pot of coffee about five minutes ago. Would you like a cup?" Viv asked.

He glanced at his watch. "How 'bout a half cup? It's almost time to open the shop."

"Perfect."

He followed her into a back room, noting the way her auburn hair shifted gently across her shoulders, the tips just brushing the collar of her green blouse.

In addition to a couple of unopened cartons of

books, the room contained a sink and a microwave on the counter with a coffeemaker next to it.

"How do you take your coffee?" she asked.

"Black's fine."

She poured coffee into a mug and handed it to him. Their eyes met for a moment in silent communication before she turned to pour coffee for herself. A ripple of awareness warned Chase that more than friendship might evolve between him and Vivian. A prospect he hadn't anticipated. Although maybe he should have.

Her hands wrapped around the mug, she leaned back against the counter. "You're a businessman. Can I ask you for some advice?" she said.

"Sure. Anything about dogs and cats and hamsters I can handle. World peace is above my pay grade."

Her laughter rang a happy note that resonated somewhere in Chase's chest.

"I promise it's nothing that earthshaking." She took a sip of her coffee. "Since the town had to cut back on its support of the library, and I lost my job there, my income has dropped considerably. I've been trying to think of a way to supplement what Allison pays me. So far I've come up empty."

"Hmm, let's see." He admired a woman who didn't sit around waiting for someone else to bail her out of trouble or take care of her. Thinking about her question, he sipped his coffee, which was rich and hot. "Maybe I could hire you to come in early to clean up the puppy pen."

She wrinkled her pert little nose. "That wasn't exactly what I had in mind."

"What were you thinking?"

"I'm not sure." She seemed pensive, as if she'd been considering the problem for some time. "If I could do something at home, then I'd be able to work around my schedule here."

"That sounds like a great idea—if you can figure it out."

"Yeah, that's a big *if*."

"It's not easy to find that kind of job." Leaning against the doorjamb, he drank some more coffee. "Telemarketing?"

Her smooth forehead furrowed. "I don't think so."

"Doing opinion polls?"

"I'm not sure I want to spend that much time on the telephone."

"Understandable." He drank another sip of coffee. "Nothing else comes immediately to mind, so let me think about it awhile."

"Sure. Maybe between us, we'll come up with something that would work."

"I'll do my best." He set his mug down on the counter. "I'd better get going."

They said their goodbyes, and Chase headed back to the pet shop, his spirits high, his footsteps light. Odd how planning an ordinary trip to an animal shelter could make him look forward to a very special day.

Because of Vivian.

When Allison arrived at the bookshop, Vivian was busily making copies of the flyer for Doggie Daze to distribute around town.

Allison picked up one of them. "This is wonderful. You're so talented. Cute dog."

"I used free clip art from the internet." Heat warmed her cheeks. "I thought this dog looked a lot like Boyo, Chase's dog."

"Oh, he does. A little bit shaggy but so cute." Allison eyed Vivian with evident curiosity. "You sure there isn't something I should know?"

"Huh? Oh, no, not really." Trying to cover the fact that she'd been so pleased to see Chase earlier, she stacked the flyers on the counter. "Chase came by early this morning. He invited me to go with him to the animal shelter tomorrow morning. If that's okay with you," she hastily added.

"Of course it's fine with me. I think it's nice we might have another romance going on here in town."

Vivian laughed self-consciously and shook her head. "I wouldn't count on that." In fact, she had to be careful not to read too much into his invitation. Chase worked closely with the shelter to help them place dogs and cats in good homes. Since Happy Endings was having the doggie event, and he no doubt had business to discuss at the shelter, it was natural that they should go together.

"I thought as long as we aren't busy, I'd deliver these flyers around town this morning," Vivian said. "And I'll drop off a few at the school and the library."

"Good idea." Allison rolled up her sleeves, ready to go to work. "Meanwhile I'll check to see what books I should order for Saturday. Maybe a couple more copies of picture books for the little ones."

"Something on training would be good," Vivian suggested. "Chase will be talking about that. And breeds of dogs."

"I'm on it." She walked into the back room, her skirt swaying at her ankles.

Since Allison's engagement to Sam, she seemed to float on air. *It must be a wonderful feeling,* Vivian mused, *to be so in love.*

A few minutes later, Vivian went out the door with an armful of flyers. She stopped at Love in Bloom first, since the flower shop was right next door.

Sherie Taylor, who worked part-time at the flower shop, came out of the back room with a vase full of yellow and purple chrysanthemums to greet her.

"Hi, Sherie. Guess you're in charge while Lily is

on her honeymoon in Canada." A slightly plump divorced mother of twins, Sherie had the kind of smile that made everyone her friend.

"I am. I'm still thrilled that she and Tate found each other."

"I think we all are." Vivian handed her a flyer, explaining what they were up to at Happy Endings and asking her to post it in the window.

Sherie agreed, putting it up as they spoke. Vivian thanked her and then went next door to Sweet Dreams Bakery.

The moment she opened the door, Vivian was met with the smell of bread baking, along with the scent of cinnamon, apples and chocolate. The aromas washed over her, and her mouth watered.

Melissa Sweeney, the owner, stood behind the counter.

"Do you know, every time I step inside here, I gain two pounds just from the sweet smell of the place?" Vivian said with a laugh. "I can feel my thighs growing by the inch."

Melissa returned her laughter in a full-throated voice. "I'd probably be a lot thinner if I'd opened a toy store instead of a bakery. I do way too much taste testing."

"Hmm, but think what we'd all miss out on right here in Bygones if you hadn't." Vivian handed Melissa a flyer, asking her if she would post it in the window. They chatted for a few minutes. Then, proud of herself for not buying one of Melissa's delicious peanut butter with chocolate drops cookies, Vivian retraced her steps, heading first to The Fixer-Upper, the new hardware store in town. After a quick visit with the very charming and recently engaged Patrick Fogerty, she was on her way again.

She'd saved Fluff & Stuff for last.

Boyo, tail wagging, met her at the door of the pet shop.

"Hi, fella. Are you keeping guard over the cash register today?" She knelt to pet him. His light brownish coat felt so silky to her; she loved to run her fingers through it.

"What's up? What's up?" the parrot announced.

"I guess guarding the cash register is Pepper's job, huh? You're just looking for some loving." As she stood, Chase arrived up front, giving her a sudden case of shyness. "Hi there."

"Hi back at ya." He grinned as his gaze swept over her simple blouse and skirt with approval. "Hope you haven't come by to cancel our trip to the animal shelter."

"Uh, no." A sharp stab of disappointment at the thought of canceling caught her off guard before she realized he was teasing. "I came by with the flyers for Doggie Daze, hoping you'd post one in your window."

"Sure will." His smile broadened like he was keeping some wonderful secret. "And I'd like some for my counter, if you have enough. I can probably talk my puppy fan club into taking some home to their parents."

"Good idea!" She gave him a handful. "If you run out, let me know. I can always print more."

Their hands brushed as he took the flyers. They stood gazing at each other for a moment. Boyo rubbing up against Chase's leg. Pepper squawking. Vivian's heart doing its pitter-patter thing in a rapid beat.

"I've got to deliver some of these to the school," she finally said, her mouth unusually dry.

"Okay, then, Viv. I'll see you in the morning."

She nodded and fled out the door, feeling like a teenager who had just been invited to the prom by the cutest boy in school.

Vivian's next delivery took her a few short blocks to the combined grammar and high school. She found Coraline Connolly, the school principal, in her office. Vivian stuck her head in the door.

"Are you busy, Mrs. Connolly?"

The older woman looked up from the stack of papers on her desk. "Not too busy to see you, Vivian. What brings you to my part of the world? Not trouble at the bookshop, I hope."

"No, not at all." In addition to being a frequent patron of the library when Vivian had worked there, Mrs. Connolly was also the heart and soul of the Save Our Streets committee, which was overseeing the revitalization of Bygones's Main Street and the new shops that had recently opened. "Allison and I have come up with an event for this Saturday. Chase of Fluff & Stuff is helping out with the idea so it can be a promotion for both of the businesses."

Taking the flyer from Vivian, Mrs. Connolly read it over. "What a good idea," she said, looking up. "I'm sure the town's benefactor would be pleased to know there is so much cooperation between our new entrepreneurs."

"Has anyone figured out yet who he, or she, is?

Mrs. Connolly lifted one shoulder in a half-hearted shrug. "Not that I'm aware of."

"Everyone is certainly curious."

"I'm sure that's true. I know I am. In any event, it's excellent that you and Allison and Chase are all working together. Chase seems to be such a nice man, and he does love his animals."

"Yes, he does." A silly flush warmed her cheeks, a problem she'd had since childhood, which she blamed on her redheaded complexion. "We're both hoping Doggie Daze not only encourages people to buy books about dogs but also helps out the Happy Havens Animal Shelter. Evidently, the shelter is strapped for both room and money with so many animals being turned over to them by families who are leaving town."

"Oh, dear, it seems like the factory closing has caused so many problems for our little town. Not the least of which is the possible closing of our school, which would force our children to be bussed to another town. Some of our teachers have already signed contracts with other districts for next semester. It's so hard to see our town suffering so." She held up the flyer and smiled, although the smile seemed a little forced. "I'll post several of these on bulletin boards around the school and hope for a good showing at Doggie Daze."

"Thanks so much." Vivian started to back out the door.

"Do give Chase my regards. It's nice to know two animal lovers will be working together for our shelter." The principal's eyes gleamed with a hint of matchmaking on her mind.

"Yes, ma'am." Flustered by the way the school principal had so easily linked her and Chase together, Vivian hurried down the hallway.

She quickly chided herself. Mrs. Connolly was only referring to their mutual concern about the shelter. She wasn't suggesting there was anything romantic going on between Vivian and Chase.

Because there wasn't.

As she walked back to Happy Endings, she passed Fluff & Stuff. Unable to help herself, she glanced inside.

Chase, who was standing by the cash register, spotted her and waved, then mouthed the words, *See you tomorrow.*

Feeling a tremble of excitement in her tummy, she waved back and gave him a thumbs-up.

What if it was possible? She and Chase? A couple?

Based on her recent experiences with men, she believed that seemed unlikely.

But what if it could be? she thought, futilely trying to still the excitement of her romantic heart.

Chapter Three

The following morning, Vivian tried on a few different outfits before settling on a shirt, with three-quarter-length sleeves, patterned in colorful fall leaves and her rust-colored skirt. She paired that with comfortable shoes for walking around the shelter, then tossed a light jacket over her arm and headed out the door.

"You be good, Essie," she called to her cat. "And leave Roger alone."

Trying to temper her eagerness as she drove into town, she still couldn't help but look forward to spending time with Chase. And, of course, visiting the shelter.

She parked on the street. By the time she reached Fluff & Stuff, Chase had already opened the door. Ready to go, he wore chinos and a tan windbreaker snug at his waist, which made his legs look extra long.

Boyo peered up at her from behind Chase's legs, his tail wagging.

"Don't you look like a bright autumn day," Chase said, ushering her inside with one of his patented grins. "Makes me think of raking leaves as a boy and jumping into the pile and then having to rake them up all over again."

"We used to do that, too. It would take us all day to finish the job. Drove our mother crazy. And then the next morning there'd be more leaves on the ground, and we'd have to do it all over again."

"My car's in back." Placing his hand at the small of her back, he guided her to the rear of the store. The heat of his palm seeped through her light jacket. "Sounds like you come from a big family," he said.

Telling Boyo to stay, Chase let Vivian out the back door and then locked it behind them.

"Mom had six kids. Three girls and three boys. We were kind of a rowdy bunch at times."

"I can imagine. Six children sounds like quite a crowd." His voice held a note of dismay. "I was an only child, which was about all my mother could handle."

"Don't tell me you misbehaved as a boy?" she asked in a teasing voice.

"Not all that much. But all kids find a way to get into trouble once in a while."

"And that was times six for my mom." Her

mother had been awesome, the most patient person Vivian knew. At least most days that was true.

When she climbed into his SUV, she caught the faint scent of puppy chow and spotted a few doggie hairs on the seat.

He went around to the driver's side and climbed behind the wheel. He seemed far more subdued than when he'd greeted her, and she couldn't imagine why. Everybody's family was different. Six children had always seemed ideal to Vivian. In fact, she'd like to have that many herself, if she could find a way.

"Is your mother still living in Wichita?" she asked quietly.

"No. She died a couple of years ago."

"I'm sorry."

He shrugged as though it didn't matter to him, but Vivian suspected he cared more about the loss of his mother than he wanted to admit. With just the two of them, they had to have been close. From Vivian's perspective, she couldn't imagine being an only child—she would have been too lonely way out on the farm. Though she admitted her younger siblings were often pests as they grew up, and she'd been expected to watch out for them when her mother was otherwise occupied.

Since their conversation had dampened Chase's mood, she decided to change the subject.

"So what kind of dogs do you think I ought to pick out for Doggie Daze?"

"We'll have to see who's available, but they should be well behaved."

"And housebroken," Vivian added. "I think Allison would appreciate that the most."

The corners of his eyes crinkled when he laughed. "I imagine so." He turned onto Bronson Street for the short drive to the shelter, which was less than a mile north of town.

Once past the center of town, houses on one- or two-acre lots replaced commercial buildings. Some families had a horse or two. Others had chicken coops and a kitchen garden, or a couple of cows grazing behind sturdy fences.

"Look at those sunflowers growing alongside the road," she said. "Aren't they beautiful?" Apparently seeds had been blown or tossed onto the right-of-way between the road and the wheat field beyond. Several hundred feet of the shoulder was ablaze with bright orange sunflowers, the Kansas state flower. Their heads on four-foot-tall stalks were all aligned, aimed directly at the sun as though they were sending cheery wishes into outer space.

"Looks like somebody decided to beautify the roadside around here."

In the distance, the silver tower of a grain elevator rose above the flat landscape, a crucial part of life for wheat farmers like Vivian's father.

"You might want to think about a bigger dog, like a golden retriever," Chase said, returning to the topic of dogs for Doggie Daze. "They're usually good with kids. And match him with something smaller, maybe a border collie mix."

"We could use a border collie to round up people off the streets to come to Doggie Daze."

He shot her an amused look. "That's one way to gain an audience. Or you could ask Police Chief Sheridan to arrest jaywalkers and hold them at the bookshop during the event."

"Or Mayor Langston could issue an edict that every resident of Bygones had to attend Doggie Daze *plus* adopt a dog at Fluff & Stuff."

They bantered back and forth, each of them coming up with more ridiculous ideas to get people to attend the event. When they pulled up in front of Happy Havens, they were both laughing so hard they could barely get out of the car.

Vivian wiped the tears from her eyes and drew a deep breath. "It's just as well we're here. I was running out of ideas."

Chase patted her hand. "I'm sure you'd be able to come up with more ideas if you had to. You're one smart lady."

She grinned at him even as the touch of his hand shot a current of warmth up her arm. "Likewise, Mr. Rollins. You're pretty smart yourself."

The shelter offices were in an old two-story

farmhouse that had been revamped and repainted a bright yellow with white trim. The adjacent red barn held most of the animals, with cats kept well separated inside the main house. Except for a small parking lot, open land and a wire fence surrounded the property. Originally funded by the Bronson family, the shelter had since been repaired and restored mostly by volunteers. Now it was entirely operated by many of those same devoted people.

In front of the house, a large sign carved in a plank of redwood read Happy Havens Animal Shelter.

Chase held open the gate, and they walked up the three steps to the porch. A note on the door invited guests to come in.

Annabelle Goodrich, wearing a navy blue windbreaker over her official shelter volunteer T-shirt, was sitting at a desk behind the counter.

"Hey, Chase, good to see you." She looked quizzically at Vivian over the top of her half-glasses. "You, too, Viv. What brings you here?"

"Viv and Allison at the bookstore are planning an event called Doggie Daze this Saturday," Chase said. "The idea is to sell books about dogs and how to train them, and hopefully get people interested in adopting dogs."

"Chase is helping us," Vivian added. "He suggested we might be able to borrow a couple of dogs from you for show-and-tell."

"And I'll need a couple for Saturday's adoption day, too," Chase added.

Lean and athletic for a woman in her fifties, Annabelle popped to her feet. "Sounds terrific. We need all the publicity we can get so our animal buddies can find new homes. Follow me." She strode toward the back of the house and on to the barn at a fast clip.

Vivian hurried to catch up with her. As she passed what must have once been the dining room, she caught a quick glimpse of a dozen or more cages containing cats. For an instant, she wanted to step inside to pick out a homeless cat and give her a new home. But she was pretty sure Essie wouldn't appreciate Vivian's generosity of spirit. Essie's nose was already out of sorts with the addition of Roger in their household.

In the barn they were greeted with a cacophony of barks and yips, and dogs jumping against their enclosure gates. Vivian could almost hear them shouting *Pick me! Pick me!* Poor fellows sure didn't like being locked up.

"Settle down, guys," Annabelle yelled over the racket. "Be nice. You need to impress these people with how well you behave." She walked down the aisle of kennels, reaching in to pet this dog and that, calling them by name and cooing over them.

Vivian caught Chase's eye. "They're her babies, aren't they?" she said quietly.

"I'd say so. Before she'll let any of them go to a new home, she checks out the family and makes it clear that if she hears about any abuse, she'll have the chief of police at their door in minutes."

"Sort of like the way they check out families when someone applies to adopt a baby," Vivian mused aloud. She had certainly filled out a lot of forms and been interviewed at length.

He shot her a troubled look. "I suppose it's the same."

Wondering why Chase would react negatively to the mention of adoption, Vivian frowned then shrugged off her concern.

Annabelle finished her tour of the kenneled dogs and returned to them. "So what kind of dogs do you want for your event?"

"Chase suggested something like a golden retriever because they're good with children," Vivian said.

Closing her eyes, Annabelle nodded. "I think I've got just the dog for you. Lady is the sweetest thing." She began walking down the aisle again. "Good family pet. Loves children. She's actually a mix of retriever and shepherd so she has a little longer nose than a pure retriever, but she's got that lovely golden fur and disposition."

She stopped at a kennel and opened the gate. "Hey, Lady. I've got someone you need to meet." She gestured for Vivian to step inside.

Vivian walked into the kennel. Immediately, Lady sat and looked up at her with intelligent brown eyes and cocked her head to the side as if waiting for Vivian to explain her presence. Vivian's heart melted.

"Aren't you the prettiest girl?" Unable to resist, she let Lady sniff her hand. Kneeling Vivian held the dog's head and gave her a good scratch behind her ears. "You are a sweetheart. You really are."

Behind her, Chase said, "I told you to be careful or you'd fall in love."

She looked up at him over her shoulder. A shimmer of awareness slid through her as she looked into his soft brown eyes filled with such a gentle spirit.

"You were…right." Her voice quavered. "I need to be very careful." And go slowly. He was talking about falling for a dog. Not him.

He helped her to her feet. "What do you think?"

Think? She didn't dare *think*. Not about Chase in that way. Not with his hand warming her arm.

"About the dog," he clarified.

"Oh, yes. Lady will be perfect for Doggie Daze." She forced a smile that felt a little crooked and turned to Annabelle. "Can we match Lady with a smaller dog she'll get along with?"

"We've got oodles of those. Let's go see Tikey. She's a sweetie." She led them to another kennel that held two small dogs. "Tikey is a Welsh corgi. Her buddy there, Arnie, is a poodle mix."

Vivian chuckled at the stumpy little dog. "It looks like Tikey didn't get her fair share of legs. They look too short for her."

"I haven't heard her complain. As Abe Lincoln once said, his legs were just the right length to reach the ground." Annabelle opened the door to let Vivian inside.

"Ol' Abe was a pretty sharp cookie," Chase commented.

It didn't take Vivian long to decide that Lady and Tikey would be perfect for show-and-tell at Doggie Daze.

Chase decided he would take Nathan for his adoption day promotion and then selected a German shepherd named Buster.

"German shepherds are well behaved and make great guard dogs," he commented. "A lot of farmers want a dog like Buster to keep an eye on their stock."

"We had a German shepherd when I was growing up." Vivian smiled at the memory. "Somewhere in the family scrapbook, there is a picture my mom took of me when I was about eighteen months old trying to ride on his back."

"Now that would be worth seeing." His dark eyes danced with mischief, and Vivian felt her cheeks heat with embarrassment.

If Chase ever met her family, she'd have to warn her mother of the dire consequences if she showed that scrapbook to him.

Unaware of Vivian's chagrin, Chase arranged with Annabelle to pick up all four dogs early Saturday morning. She promised to have them bathed and ready to go by eight o'clock.

Annabelle walked with them to the barn's entrance. "Mayor Langston dropped by a day or two ago. We got to talking about the shelter and how there simply aren't enough funds to keep this place going for long."

"Oh, I'm sorry hear that," Vivian said. "Is there anything anyone can do to help?"

Wrinkles furrowed Annabelle's forehead as she fussed with the zipper on her jacket. "The mayor and I were trying to come up with some sort of a fund-raiser that would keep us going. Nothing came to mind right offhand. But if you think of something…" She let the words drift off on the weight of her concern.

"We'll give it some thought," Chase promised, ushering Vivian out the door.

Walking slowly, Vivian considered the shelter's financial problem. It would be such a shame to have to close it down. There had to be something….

Back in the SUV, Chase turned to her. "It's almost noon. How about I drive us to Highway 135? We can have lunch at the Red Rooster diner."

"That sounds good, but don't you have to open up your shop? Or did you have your friend open for you?"

"Midweek isn't a problem. I left a sign on my door that I'd be back by two o'clock. I don't get much business in the mornings, especially during the middle of the week, so I'm not losing any sales to speak of."

"Then it's fine with me. Allison told me to take as much time as I needed at the shelter." Although she hadn't said anything about having lunch with Chase.

Buckling her seat belt, Vivian felt a tickle of pleasure that she'd be spending more time with him.

He started the car and shifted into Reverse to back out of the parking place. "Someday soon, if and when my business picks up a bit, I'm going to have to hire someone part-time so I can be away from the store when I need to leave. The Save Our Streets committee is putting together a list of local folks who are looking for work. They want us to hire from that list if we can. I'm thinking that as Christmas gets closer, I'll take a look. I'm told there are some hard workers on the list."

"Yes, you should have someone to help, and it would be wonderful if you could hire someone local. With me helping at the bookshop, Allison has some flexibility she wouldn't have otherwise."

There weren't many cars on the two-lane country road that led to the highway. Once Chase had to go around a slow-moving tractor, the farmer probably planning to disk his fields for the winter so they'd be ready for planting come spring. Vivian's father, who grew wheat on his acreage near Duncan Springs, had already prepared the ground for winter.

"So why did you decide to be a librarian?" Chase asked as they were driving along.

"I love books," she replied easily. "I grew up with my nose in a book since as early as I can remember. My older sister Lisa was very outgoing, but I'd hide in my room or in the loft of the barn and read. Guess I was just shy."

He glanced in her direction. "You don't seem very shy now. In fact, you've got a great personality."

"Thanks." Pleased that Chase saw her in such a positive light, she gave him an appreciative smile. "When I went off to college, I decided I had to become more extroverted. So I intentionally joined a bunch of clubs, volunteered for various activities. I didn't want to be the stereotypical meek, bookish librarian."

"I'd say you achieved your goal. You're definitely not a stereotype at all. You're one of a kind."

"Careful, Chase. You're going to have me blushing with all your compliments." And falling for him harder and faster than she should.

"Not to worry. I like it when your cheeks turn pink. The color is good with your hair."

She rolled her eyes. Blushing was the bane of every redhead she knew. She so hoped he wasn't giving her a line just to make points with her. "I may have learned to be more outgoing, but I'm still a bookworm at heart."

They arrived at the diner, which had a gigantic red rooster perched on top of the sloping roof. Several cars and trucks were parked in the lot, and Chase had to drive around to the back to find an open slot.

"Busy place," she commented.

"As nearly as I can tell, it's the only decent diner between Newton and Highway 40."

"True. I'm afraid this part of Kansas isn't exactly the gourmet capital of the state."

They got out of the car and strolled around to the entrance. Inside the smell of sizzling meat on the grill was accompanied by a pleasant hum of conversation from the patrons who filled the red vinyl booths. Waitresses hurried back and forth carrying trays of burgers and fries, cold sandwiches and salads, plus glasses of soda and iced tea.

The hostess showed them to a booth toward the back of the restaurant.

Vivian opened the menu the hostess had placed

in front of her. "So are you into gourmet food?" she asked Chase. "Or are you more a meat-and-potatoes kind of guy?"

"I'm a pretty basic guy. No frills. You get what you see."

What Vivian saw in Chase was looking better and better. "I don't mind going out to a fancy dinner now and then, but my mom taught me to cook. Chicken and biscuits is about as wild as we get in my family. But Mom's biscuits are pretty good."

He studied her from across the table. "I'm a serious connoisseur of biscuits. I like 'em real fluffy."

"Well, good. In that case I'll have to invite you to dinner at my folks' house sometime so you can see if Mom's biscuits live up to your high standards."

He chuckled. "It's a deal!"

When the waitress returned, Chase ordered a cheeseburger with coleslaw instead of fries. Vivian chose a chicken salad with a raspberry vinaigrette dressing on the side. She had iced tea; he ordered a soda.

As they chatted over lunch, Vivian learned Chase had grown up in Wichita, living in a half dozen different houses or apartments. And that he'd started work at a warehouse when he was seventeen years old.

"You didn't want to go to college?" she asked.

"My grades weren't good enough, and I had to earn some money to help out my mother."

Vivian sensed he was plenty smart enough to get good grades and go to college, but maybe he hadn't been tuned in to academics. Some of her classmates had been like that: smart but not interested in studying. Then again, given his family's situation, maybe he hadn't had any other choice.

She sipped her sweet tea. "What about your interests outside of animals? Any hobbies?"

Thinking, he carried a forkful of coleslaw to his mouth and chewed for a minute. "When I was younger, I used to enjoy target practice with some buddies. They sometimes went hunting, but I couldn't see killing a deer or even a raccoon."

"Neither can I." Her father had a gun, which he used to run off coyotes who were trying to get into the chicken coup. But Vivian had never been interested in shooting anything, not even a target.

"Like most guys, I've tinkered a little with cars," Chase said. "How about you? What do you do in your spare time?"

"You mean besides reading?" She laughed. "I can do some crocheting and knitting, but I'm not all that good. My mother's terrific, though. I'm pretty good at graphic arts on the computer. And I like decorating my little house."

"On the computer, it's all I can do to keep track of income, expenses and inventory. I bought a special program for that. Figured I'd need it come tax season."

"Smart man." She smiled at him across the table and felt herself falling further for this man.

When they'd finished eating, Vivian sat back. "That was a good salad. I'll have to come here more often."

"Good burger, too." Using his napkin, Chase wiped his mouth. "We'll have to do this again."

Their waitress arrived. She was a woman in her forties with unnatural platinum hair pulled back into a ponytail. "Anything else for you folks? We've got some homemade apple pie. It's really good à la mode."

Vivian shook her head. "Not for me, thanks."

"None for me, either." The waitress put the check on the table, and Chase reached for his wallet.

"Why don't we do this Dutch treat?" Vivian suggested.

"A gentleman never lets a lady pick up the check." He put a twenty on the table. "I invited you, remember."

"Well, I thank you very much."

He winked. "You're welcome."

"Guess we'd better get back to work, huh?" Although Vivian would rather linger here with Chase, sipping another glass of iced tea, she really should go to the bookstore to give Allison a break.

Chase took a different road back to Bygones, although the landscape of small farms was much the same. They hadn't gone far when he had to slow for a couple of brown-and-white milk cows that had wandered out onto the road.

"Looks like somebody left their gate open," Vivian said.

"No, not their gate." He pulled to the side of the road. "A whole big section of fencing is down."

"How did that happen?" Two posts holding the wire fencing around a small pasture had been pulled to the ground. The cows had simply wandered out to eat the greener grass outside their pen.

Turning off the ignition, Chase said, "I'm going to try to herd the cows back where they belong. The farmer must not have missed them yet. Hang on." He hopped out of the SUV and strolled slowly toward the cows.

Vivian climbed out, too. There was a small farmhouse and a barn on the property, both of which looked in need of a new roof and fresh paint. That wasn't unusual in this part of Kansas. Small landholders had trouble making a profit.

"Come on, Bessie," Chase said. "You and your sister need to go back where you came from." Making clucking noises, he waved them toward the broken fence.

The cows started to move in the right direction.

Suddenly an old man half bent over at the waist came running out of the house. "Hey there, git away from my cows, or I'll blow you away." The man lifted a double-barrel shotgun to his shoulder.

Vivian gasped.

Chase threw his hands up. "Easy, mister. You've got a break in your fence. I was just trying to—"

The shotgun blasted into the air. "I tol' you to git. Now git!" He cracked open the shotgun, reloaded and snapped it closed.

The cows lumbered out onto the road again.

Her heart in her throat, Vivian jumped back in the SUV, rolling down her window.

Chase, instead of getting into the truck and driving away, like any rational person would do, walked toward the farmer, his hands held out to his sides in a sign of peace.

"Be careful," she whispered, appalled that he'd approach a man with a gun.

"I'd like to help you," Chase told the farmer. "I live over in Bygones. I own the pet store. I know what it's like to work hard and not have much to show for it."

Slowly, the farmer lowered his shotgun an inch or two. "Kids are always messing with my cows. When hunting season started, one of 'em painted a red target on Marshmallow."

"I'm sorry. I really am. Kids can do stupid things."

Her heart in her throat, Vivian watched as Chase kept moving closer to the farmer. If the farmer lifted that shotgun again and pulled the trigger, Chase could be dead in minutes.

Please, God. Don't let anything bad happen to him. She pulled out her cell phone, ready to call for help.

"How about I try to bring Marshmallow back where she belongs? Then you and I can brace that fence back up. What do you say, Mr....?"

"Mahnken. Amos Mahnken."

"Good to meet you, Amos." He extended his hand. "Chase Rollins."

Switching the shotgun to his left hand, Amos took Chase's hand. "You'll need a switch. Marshmallow needs a little flick now and again to get her moving. Brownie usually follows along all right."

Vivian exhaled the breath she'd been holding. Chase was either crazy or extremely brave. Maybe both, she thought, hysteria threatening.

"I'll get her." Reaching for a dry weed stalk, Chase broke it off. "You go find us some wood and a hammer and nails. This shouldn't take long."

Shaking, Vivian waited in the truck while Chase rounded up the cows, then helped Amos restore the fence to some order.

Finally, Chase told Amos goodbye. They shook hands like old friends, and Chase returned to the SUV.

"Sorry for the delay," he said, climbing behind the wheel.

"Sorry?" She nearly choked. "You could've been *killed!*"

"Naw. Old Amos didn't want to kill anybody. Just wanted to scare me off."

"Well, he certainly scared me. Right out of ten years of my life."

Looking at her, he cocked his head. A little smile played around his lips. "Thanks for worrying about me."

He tucked a wayward strand of hair behind her ear, then he shifted the SUV into gear and pulled back onto the road.

Her cheek tingled with the residual warmth of his fingertip. Her heart beating hard, all Vivian could do was gape at the man. Maybe she was the one who was crazy.

Because she was thinking about crazy, exciting possibilities and dreams that could come true.

Chapter Four

With Amos Mahnken's farm well behind him in the rearview mirror, Chase glanced at Vivian. Sitting next to him, she had her hands clasped tightly in her lap, and she was staring out the windshield. Slight grooves creased her forehead.

"You all right?" he asked. Viv looked as tense as someone staring down a bull on a rampage, his big horns leveled right at her.

"I'm fine," she said too brightly. "I think my heart rate ought to slow down by tomorrow afternoon or thereabouts."

He grinned, wondering if her reaction had been to his impulsive touch of her hair. Or the fact that old Amos had fired his shotgun. Poor guy had probably scared himself as much as he had scared Chase.

"I have no idea how you had the nerve to face him down with a gun in his hands," Viv said.

"I don't know. I guess I figured the guy needed help, and it didn't look like there was anyone around to bail him out of trouble. He's too old to be digging postholes on his own. It seemed natural to try to give him a hand."

"You're a true gentleman, Chase Rollins. And very kind."

He snorted, embarrassed by her compliment. "While we were fixing the fence, I spotted something that bothered me. There were tire tracks by the fence. Looked to me like someone had intentionally pulled that fence down."

Viv's head swiveled toward him. "Why would anyone want to do that?"

"I don't know. But there's been some vandalism going on around Bygones. I'm sure Allison told you about the last meeting of the new shopkeepers. Everyone was talking about an increase in someone breaking things and spray painting stuff. I think Amos could be the most recent victim."

"Allison and I did talk after the meeting about how Elwood was quite upset about what happened at The Everything, with picnic tables being tossed around in the wee hours of the morning and a window broken."

"Right. And Brian Montclair had some tools stolen, even though they were eventually found. Maybe it's getting more serious. If a vandal pulled down

Amos's fence, and Marshmallow or Brownie got hit by a truck, it would've cost the old guy plenty."

Chase turned at the intersection of Bronson, heading into town.

"Maybe your friend Amos could use a big dog like Buster to run off vandals and trespassers."

His lips crept into a smile at her suggestion. "You're right. Like I said, you're one smart, clever lady." Pretty, too, but he didn't want to embarrass her more than he already had. "Maybe I'll run out there after Saturday's adoption day to see if I can talk him into that."

"Finding a home for Buster would be great."

Chase thought so, too, as he pulled up in front of Happy Endings Bookstore. "Back to the ol' grind, I'm afraid."

"Working in a bookstore would never be a grind for me." She popped open her car door. "Thanks for taking me to the shelter and to lunch. I enjoyed it."

"We'll do it again sometime. I take all my dates to an animal shelter. It's my favorite thing to do." He nearly bit his tongue when he realized he'd referred to their outing as a date. He really didn't want her to get the wrong idea.

"Oh, you…" Laughing, she got out of his SUV, waved goodbye and hurried into bookstore.

Chase drove slowly away, around the block to park in his enclosed backyard. He'd enjoyed Viv's company a lot. Probably more than he should. As long as he kept thinking of her as a *friend,* there'd be no problems. He didn't want to risk a deeper relationship.

For about a year in Wichita he'd been dating a woman he had liked a lot. But then she had laid down the law: either they get married and start a family or it's over.

He chose to break off their relationship.

Because he was never going to take a chance on being a father himself. With the genes he carried, those terrible traits handed down by his own abusive alcoholic father, he knew that was a deal breaker. For the woman.

And for any child he might father.

Not long after Chase opened the pet store, Elwood Dill, the owner of The Everything store and Chase's contact with the Save Our Streets committee, showed up.

The moment Elwood stepped in the shop, his scraggly beard showing touches of gray and his tie-dyed T-shirt sporting what looked like ketchup stains, Pepper had a fit.

"Bad Birdie! Bad Birdie! Polly's not here! Polly's not here!"

Laughing, Chase told the bird to hush up.

"Hey, Elwood. What's up?" he asked.

"What's up? What's up?" Using his beak, Pepper

jingled like crazy the string of tiny silver bells in his cage.

Boyo trotted over to see what was going on.

"Stop showing off, Pepper." Chase waved Elwood toward the back of the store. "Let's get away from that crazy bird. Unless I can talk you into buying him?" Although, given Pepper's vocabulary, he had to be pretty smart. A real prize for someone.

"He sure would liven up my store, but I think I'll pass. Thanks anyway."

"Pity. I think Pepper would fit right in with your customers."

Elwood shot him scathing look. "Nothing's wrong with my customers."

"Of course not." Chase gave him an affectionate slap on the back.

They strolled out of Pepper's sight behind a display that featured leashes, collars and assorted doggie toys.

"I have to admit, Pepper isn't the fastest moving item I've got in stock," Chase said. "I may be stuck with him for a long time." Which, when he thought about it, didn't seem like a terrible idea.

"I've got some stuff at The Everything that Velma and I picked up before we were married, and I still haven't been able to move it."

Since Elwood and his wife were both in their fifties, Chase figured if Elwood didn't get that merchandise sold soon, it would turn into antiques and be worth a small fortune.

Elwood examined a dog collar studded with fake gemstones. "You know what, Chase? Your displays are too neat. It's a fine line, but you need just a touch of clutter." He waved his hand back and forth across the items for sale. "Folks like to think people have been pawing through things 'cause the stuff is such a good buy. If you keep your merchandise too neat and tidy, people are afraid to mess things up. So they don't even take a look."

Chase suppressed a smile. "That's an interesting marketing philosophy."

"Yep. I've been in business here in Bygones a long time and know what works. You might want to give it a try."

"I'll think about it." *For less than a second.* Clutter wasn't Chase's style.

"Anyway…" Elwood hung the collar back on the display peg. "I came by to see how you're doing, and to remind you we are not going to have an SOS meeting until next week. A couple of folks have other commitments they couldn't break."

The Save Our Streets meeting was a way for the new shopkeepers to make any problems, or successes, known to the others. "That makes sense. She'd want to keep up with whatever went on while she was gone."

"Yep. That's what we all figured." He headed for the front door, Chase and Boyo right behind him.

"By the way," Chase said. "I stumbled across what might be the latest case of vandalism." He explained about Amos's fence being pulled down and the cows escaping.

Scratching his long beard, Elwood nodded. "I sure wish Chief Sheridan hadn't had to let so many police officers go. We need somebody out there tracking this vandal down before something awful happens."

"You've got that right." Chase picked up one of the flyers from the counter. "I've got my monthly animal adoption day coming up this Saturday, and Happy Endings has a special Doggie Daze going on, too."

Taking the flyer, Elwood scanned it quickly. "Vivian brought a bunch of flyers by yesterday for Doggie Daze. I've got 'em posted."

"Good birdie," Pepper crooned.

"You sure you don't want a parrot? Pepper seems quite taken with you."

Laughing in a deep baritone voice, Elwood shook his head. "And I don't want you trying to talk Velma into buying that bird, either. She does enough talking all by herself. I don't need any more chatter going on in the shop."

Smiling, Chase held open the door as Elwood

left. One of these days somebody would come along who wouldn't be able to resist Pepper. Soon, he hoped.

That evening, still upbeat from lunch with Chase, Vivian baked a chicken breast for dinner and tossed a small salad. She ate her meal while watching the news, then sat on her couch to read.

She had borrowed *Mystery at Mercer Point* from the bookshop a couple of days ago and was eager to finish the story. The author, Marilee Davis, lived in Arkansas and had become one of Vivian's favorite writers. So far Davis had authored three books, but she hadn't moved up on the lists to bestsellerdom as yet. Vivian thought Marilee was due.

Essie hopped up into Vivian's lap, stomped down a nest and settled in for the duration.

"Do make yourself comfortable." Vivian stroked Essie, smoothing her soft fur, then opened the book.

"You know, sometimes I think heartland authors get short shrift from New York's opinion makers. It's like the whole center of the country is ignored by the literati."

Holding the book in one hand and petting the cat with the other, she read several pages, loving Davis's wordsmithing and the clever way she dropped in the clues, leading to the culprit who had stolen the antique brass andirons from Mrs. Murphy, the wealthiest woman in the town of Mercer Point.

Frowning, an idea teasing at her brain, Vivian marked her place and slowly closed the book.

"You know what this author needs? More publicity, that's what. She's writing for such a small publisher, she needs to find a way to get more recognition. More buzz about her books."

She eased Essie out of her lap and went to her laptop, which sat on the kitchen table. As she booted it up, she wondered if it would be possible for her to earn some extra money writing a regular blog about the books she loved.

Would it be enough money to make her more acceptable as a single parent to an adoption agency?

By Saturday morning, Vivian had researched blogs, how they attracted advertising and had a title for her book blog: Heartland Musings, Heartland Authors and Their Books. She even had created a design for her home page. She'd concentrate on small regional publishers and their books. She couldn't take money from publishers to review their books. That wouldn't be ethical. But she could search out other businesses that had an interest in Midwestern markets.

It might take time to build a following, and the income that went with it, but she didn't want to simply wait around until every agency had turned down her application to adopt a child because she didn't earn enough money to support one.

Getting the ball rolling, she'd at least be able to show that she had a plan for herself and her baby's financial future.

But for now, she needed to put aside thoughts of her blog and focus on Doggie Daze.

Before they had left work last night, she and Allison had rearranged the Kids' Korner to make more room to display dog-related books and show off Lady and Tikey, the stars of the event.

First thing this morning, Vivian had set out a plate of cookies she'd picked up from Sweet Dreams Bakery next door.

"I sure wish we knew how many people were coming today," she said to Allison.

Carrying a pitcher of punch, Allison came out of the back room. "I have plenty of extra punch if we need it." She placed the pitcher on the counter next to the cookies.

"So if no one comes, we can drown our sorrows in cookies and punch," Vivian joked.

"Let's hope it doesn't come to that." Allison checked her watch. "What time do you think Chase will be here with the dogs?"

"Any minute now." At the mention of Chase's name, Vivian's heart did a little flip. She hadn't seen him since their trip to the shelter. But she hadn't stopped thinking about him, either.

Under usual circumstances, a trip to an animal shelter plus a lunch together wouldn't add up to much. But something about Chase drew her. Made her want a connection with him. Gave her hope.

As predicted, within a few minutes Chase knocked on the door. Slightly breathless, Vivian opened it for him.

Lady nearly bowled her over, she was so eager to get inside. With her tail wagging at the speed of light, so fast it was little more than a blur, the retriever pulled hard on the leash Chase was holding. Her tongue lolled out the side of her mouth.

"Lady, heel!" Chase ordered.

It did no good.

Vivian dropped onto her knees to hug the dog, and scratch her around her ears and shoulders. "Didn't Annabelle tell you that you had to be well behaved today?"

Lady licked her face.

"I don't think Lady got the memo," Chase said, still clinging to Lady's leash. Meanwhile, Tikey, also on a leash, had poked her head in the doorway, looking around cautiously.

Standing, Vivian said, "Just as well this isn't a china and glass shop. Lady's tail alone would cost the owner a fortune in broken merchandise."

A frown tugged a V between Chase's brows. "Do you think you can handle her?"

"Hopefully she'll calm down before any kids and their parents show up." She took the leash and tugged on Lady's harness. "Lady, sit." She gestured with her hand, showing the dog what she wanted.

Lady sat, although her tail and tongue kept up their perpetual motion. She looked ready to leap up and race around the room with the least little encouragement.

"Impressive." Chase's eyes sparked with admiration as he smiled at Vivian. "At least you got her to sit. She was all over my SUV on the way back to town."

Allison joined them at the entry. "These are our two charmers?"

"Meet Lady and Tikey," Vivian said. "Lady is pretty excited right now."

"I would be, too, if I'd been kept at an animal shelter for days and had finally gotten out." Kneeling, Allison greeted Tikey. "Now, she's a shy one, isn't she?" She took Tikey's leash from Chase.

"She's shy for now, anyway," Chase said. "I hope they both behave themselves."

"They'll be fine," Vivian reassured both Chase and Allison. "How 'bout your dogs for adoption day?"

"Henry's letting them run around in the yard behind the shop for a bit. Use up some of their energy."

Vivian wondered if they should do the same with Lady and Tikey.

"What time do you want me to come over to talk about breeds and training?" Chase asked.

"Our flyer says we start at ten. By ten-thirty everyone ought to be here that's coming," Allison said. "We'll give them some time to pet the dogs and get acquainted before you come over."

"Okay, I'll be here at ten-thirty." His gaze met Vivian's. "Good luck. Hope everything works out!"

"Thanks. We might need it. Hope you find homes for Buster and Nathan."

"I do, too." He stepped back then turned, heading to his own shop.

Vivian closed the door.

"I'd say that gentleman is seriously attracted to you," Allison commented. "I think I saw a gleam in his eye."

"We'll see. Besides, you're probably imagining things," Vivian responded lightly with a toss of her hair and hoped her blush wasn't too obvious. "Right now we'd better figure out how we're going to handle these two dogs."

Chase arrived at Happy Endings on time as promised. His audience consisted of a dozen youngsters, ages four to ten, and eight parents. A nice turnout for Doggie Daze.

Allison introduced him to the group. And for the next half hour, Vivian admired Chase as he talked about dogs. His love for them shone as bright as the North Star on a clear winter night in Kansas.

His connection with the children was quite amazing. He got down to the level of a four-year-old to explain why Tikey had such short legs.

"Just like you got your blond hair from your mom and dad, Tikey got her short legs from her mom and dad. Tikey's really smart, and she likes to herd other animals like sheep."

"Would she herd my cat?" the little boy asked, his eyes big, round circles of bright blue.

Chase hesitated a moment but kept a straight face. "Cats are really hard to herd, so I don't think so. But she'd be very loyal to a little boy, like you, and follow him around all the time."

The boy looked up at his mother. "Could we get Tikey, Mommy? She could be my friend."

The boy's mother looked helpless in the face of such a touching plea. "We'll talk about it later, sweetheart."

"Pleeaassee," the boy pleaded.

Suppressing a smile, Vivian hoped that Tikey had found a fine new home.

Whitney Leigh, the reporter for the *Bygones Gazette,* had slipped into the bookstore during the presentation. A young, attractive blonde, she wore her hair back in a bun. Oversize glasses hid her green eyes as she snapped a few photos and took notes.

From across the room, she winked at Vivian and

shot her a thumbs-up. Then she quietly exited via the back door. Vivian imagined there would be a nice story in the next edition of the paper.

When Chase finished his talk and demonstration, Allison invited the group to examine the books on display, and Vivian manned the cash register. Chase lingered awhile to visit with a couple of families who had questions.

As the crowd thinned, Allison joined Vivian behind the counter. "This has been wonderful. I so appreciate what you and Chase have done to make Doggie Daze a success."

"It's been fun, and we sold a lot of books. I think we ought to repeat Doggie Daze again next year."

"I do, too," Allison agreed. "And to celebrate our success, I'd like to invite you and Chase to dinner tonight. I'm cooking spaghetti at Sam's house. It's the twins' favorite. All very informal." She chuckled. "As if with the twins we could have dinner any other way."

"I'd love to come. But I'll have to check with Chase. I have no idea what his plans are." For all Vivian knew, he could be seeing someone in Wichita. They hadn't talked about personal relationships, past or present, not that she had anything like that going on herself.

Allison indicated that would be fine and went off to help one of the fathers who was browsing in the mystery section.

When Chase finished talking with the four-year-old's mother, he brought Lady and Tikey to the front of the bookstore and stopped at the counter.

"Looks like Tikey has found a new home," he said under his breath, grinning. "Mom is going to visit the shelter on Monday."

"That's wonderful. I'm so glad," Vivian whispered. "I hope she doesn't back out."

"She'd suffer a historic tantrum from her little boy if she did."

"Oh, dear, she wouldn't want that." Vivian sputtered a laugh.

"I've got to get these guys back to Fluff & Stuff and see how Henry's doing."

"Wait a minute." She touched his arm. "Allison wants us both to come to dinner tonight. She's cooking dinner at Sam's house. Spaghetti."

His eyebrows rose in surprise. "That sounds great. I could use some home cooking. I'll have to take the dogs back to the shelter first, though."

"I'm sure that will be fine. I'll have to go home to change, anyway. Allison says it's casual."

"I could pick you up, and we could go together," he offered.

Her heart did a rat-a-tat-tat and fingertips of excitement tingled down her spine. "I'd like that. I live a little ways out of town, but my house isn't hard to find." She gave him the directions.

"I'll be there about six."

"I'll tell Allison we're both on for dinner."

Vivian watched him go out the door, a smile bubbling up inside her until it spread to her lips. She didn't care if this was Allison's way of playing matchmaker. All she cared about was that Chase had accepted the dinner invitation, and they were going together.

Chapter Five

Chase pulled up in front of the small house at the edge of an abandoned wheat farm. The porch light cast a welcoming glow, revealing two wicker chairs for anyone who might want to sit and watch a sunset. He could imagine a pleasant summer interlude with Viv, sitting there at the end of a long day and quietly enjoying each other's company.

An interesting image, he realized, but one that wasn't going to happen.

As he walked up to the porch, a calico cat peered out between the curtains of the picture window. Viv's cat, Essie, he thought with a smile, and knocked on the door. The cat vanished from the window.

After a moment's wait, he heard Vivian unbolt the door and pull it open.

"Hi there," she said breathlessly. "You're right on time."

"Hi yourself." Her vibrancy and healthy glow were amplified by her bright red top. Her feet were bare, the nails painted the same shade as her top. "I like that shirt on you. It brings out your blue eyes. Nice toenail polish, too."

"Thanks." His compliment brought the hint of color to her cheeks. "Come on in. I've got to get my shoes." She took a step back.

As he walked inside, he said, "I've come bearing good news."

"Oh?"

Proud of his success, he said, "Buster has a new home. Amos has a new buddy."

"That's wonderful!" Vivian threw herself at him, startling Chase as she wrapped her arms around his neck. She felt good as he returned her hug; she was slender yet feminine, almost petite in her bare feet, and he caught the tangy citrus scent of her shampoo.

Cautiously, she backed out of their embrace. Her eyes danced with excitement. "I'm so glad and happy for Buster."

He instantly missed the soft warmth of her body against his. "I'm happy for Amos, too. He's been widowed a couple of years, and his kids have moved away. I don't think they visit very often. I suspect he's been really lonely."

"It's so thoughtful of you to think of Amos needing a doggie friend."

"Remember it was your idea, so you're the thoughtful one. I'm just the delivery boy. I cleared everything with Annabelle when I took the show-and-tell dogs back to the shelter. I wish all the shelter placements were such a good match."

"Me, too. And you're a lot more than a delivery boy." Her smile warmed an empty place in Chase's chest. He had the urge to pull her into his arms again and kiss her rosy lips. "Give me a sec while I get my shoes on. Then we can go."

She vanished into her bedroom, and he glanced around the living room. Everything was neat and tidy, the colors bright and inviting. He spotted Essie, who was perched on the back of the couch and was eyeing him with more than a little curiosity.

"Hey there, Essie. It's nice to meet you." He moved slowly to the couch and sat down near the cat. "Would you let me pet you? I'm a pretty nice guy when you get to know me."

Her tail switched once. Her yellow eyes remained fixed on him, wary yet intrigued. The tip of her pink tongue peeked out.

Slowly he eased his hand along the back of the couch to let Essie catch his scent. "You'll probably smell Boyo and Fluff on me. Maybe you'll meet them in person someday." When Essie didn't object to his presence, he gave her a gentle scratch under the chin, which elicited a soft purr.

"I think she likes you," Viv said from behind

him. "Sometimes she can be a little tentative with strangers."

"She's responding to my undeniably charming personality."

"You're pretty cocky, aren't you?" she said with a chuckle.

"Or more likely it's the fact that she can smell Boyo and Fluff on me and figures I can't be all bad." He stood. "Ready to go?"

"I am. Unless you'd like to say hello to Roger."

"Sure, why not?"

She took him into the spare bedroom, where Roger's cage sat on top of a desk. The moment the hamster spotted Chase, he made a dash for his house in the corner of his cage.

"Hey, Roger. Don't you remember I was the one who found you such a good home?" Chase strolled over to the cage and opened the door. He reached inside to snare Roger.

The animal's nose quivered as he caught Chase's scent. Only then did Roger settle down enough to be petted.

"Yeah, I thought you'd remember me." Chase nuzzled the guinea pig then put him back in his little house.

"You're really good with animals," Viv commented. "Have you ever thought of opening a pet store?"

"Say, now, that's a good idea. I just might do

that." He caught the teasing glint in her eyes and felt a lifting of his heart. He couldn't remember the last time a woman had made him feel so good, so manly, as Viv did just by being with him. He loved the way they could tease back and forth. Her quick wit. And how her smile seemed directed at him alone.

He hadn't felt the same way about the woman he'd been dating in Wichita. Viv was simply more fun to be with than she had been, and he wondered why he hadn't recognized that at the time.

He helped Viv into her jacket, which gave him another chance to be close to her and catch the hint of citrus in her hair.

Chase had gotten directions to Sam Franklin's home from Allison. The high school basketball coach lived just outside of downtown in a two-story Victorian featuring gingerbread trim and a large yard with lots of trees. In the center of the yard stood a swing set for Sam's three-year-old twins. Chase parked at the curb right in front.

"This is a lovely old house," Viv said as she climbed out of the SUV.

"Looks like Sam has kept it well maintained." Chase took her arm as they walked up to the porch. "I understand Sam and his ex-wife, who left him a couple of years ago, had bought the house together. When they split, he got the house. Now he pretty much has full custody of the twins, too."

"Marriages can be tough going." From what he knew of Sam, he counted the basketball coach as one of the good guys. In any event, divorce was hard on everyone involved. Even when it was the smartest thing Chase's mother had ever done to escape his father, it had still been hard on her. She'd always harbored guilt that the beatings and divorce had been her fault. Which Chase knew wasn't true at all.

"Allison is so blessed to have found Sam. I'd give my right arm to live in a house like this," Viv said.

"I'd rather you didn't risk your arm." He gave it a squeeze. "I'm rather fond of your arms. Both of them."

She cut him a sideways look just as the front door opened.

"You made it!" Allison opened the door wide. "Come in. Come in. We're so glad you could join us for dinner."

The thunder of little feet pounded into the entryway, and two very short people appeared, Nicholas and Rosalie.

Allison extended her hand to slow their arrival. "Easy, kids. You remember Chase Rollins, who owns the pet store? And you know Vivian, who helps me at the bookstore. This is Rosie and Nicky." She touched the top of each head as she reintroduced the twins.

"Hi, kids." Chase gave them a finger wave.

"Can you say hello?" Allison asked the children. Two sets of brown eyes stared up at Chase.

"Hello," Rosie piped up in a strong voice.

"Can we eat now?" Nicky asked. "I'm hungry."

"Ah, a young man after my own heart," Chase said.

Suppressing a smile, Allison cupped the back of Nicky's head. "Why don't we let our guests in the door and give them a chance to take off their jackets? Then we can eat."

As though on matching spindles, the twins whirled and raced back the way they had come. They were replaced by Sam, who ushered Chase and Vivian inside.

"You've got to forgive my kids," he said. "There's something about the vitamins these days that make them like little dynamos."

"They're adorable." Stepping inside, Viv slipped out of her jacket and handed it to Allison. "And I love your house. It's like a storybook place."

"Nowadays, Allison is in charge of all the storybooks around here." Sam, a big athletic man, gave Chase a firm handshake and a guy-style slap on his shoulder.

Even from the entry, Chase could smell the scent of tomato sauce laced with oregano coming from the kitchen, and his mouth watered.

"I hear Doggie Daze went well this morning.

One of the dogs might've found a home, too." Sam gestured them into the living room.

A dark leather couch and love seat were arranged to take full advantage of a low fire burning in the brick fireplace. Above it, decorative items were neatly displayed on the oak mantel. A dark oak coffee table matched the two side tables beside the couch and love seat. The furniture sat on an area rug in shades of brown and blue, the hardwood floor visible around the border.

Chase found himself envying Sam and his comfortable home, a place much larger and nicer than any he'd ever lived in. He'd used most of the money he'd saved from the warehouse job to buy into the pet store and build up his stock of merchandise. It would be a long time before he'd be able to move out of the upstairs apartment. Although he figured there was no rush. It was fine for him on his own.

He glanced at Viv, who was talking with Allison. A woman needed more than a one-bedroom apartment over a pet store to call her own. She needed enough room to turn it into a home.

Chase sat on the love seat and Sam on the couch, and Viv went into the kitchen to help Allison with the finishing touches for dinner.

"I've heard the school may have to close at the end of the term," Chase commented.

"It's entirely possible."

"So where would that leave you? And your athletes?"

Sam shrugged, an easy lift of his shoulders that Chase didn't quite believe. "Looking for another job, which isn't easy at midterm. I did get an offer from a school in Florida, but I don't want to leave Bygones." His gaze shifted to Allison and he smiled. All the kids will be going to different schools, so the teams will likely be broken up. They'll have to compete with existing players for a spot on the teams. It'll be tough for them."

Chase imagined so, even though he'd never played on a school sports team. There'd never been enough time for him to pursue athletics.

The twins reappeared in the living room. Chocolate circled both of their mouths, suggesting they'd gotten a snack to keep them going until dinner.

They planted themselves right in front of Chase.

"I'm three years old," Rosie confessed.

"You're getting to be a big girl," Chase responded with a quick look at Sam.

"I'm big, too," Nicky announced.

Chase shifted his attention to the boy. "I can see that."

"How old are you?" Rosie asked.

Chase swallowed a chuckle. "A lot older than three."

"Are you older than Daddy?"

"Uh, I don't know. We're about the same, I guess." Though Chase figured he had a couple of years on Sam. And Sam looked to be in far better shape, probably because he worked out with his basketball players.

Rosie contemplated his answer for a moment, her tiny forehead furrowing. "My daddy's old."

Chase choked on a laugh at the same time Sam got up from his chair and scooped his daughter into his arms. "That's enough interrogation for now, Rosie."

Fortunately, Allison called dinner, which Chase suspected saved Sam from explaining what *interrogation* meant.

After a heated discussion between the twins as to who would sit where, they all sat down at a large oak table in the formal dining room. A child flanked both Sam and Allison. Chase and Viv were seated next to each other.

"Sam, will you say grace for us?" Allison asked.

Caught off guard for a moment, Chase lowered his head. Saying grace at mealtime hadn't been a part of his life.

Viv took one of Sam's hands and Rosie grabbed the other. The child's sticky fingers felt small and trusting. Viv's hand fit perfectly in his.

"Dear Lord," Sam began. "Thank You for the food we are about to eat and for the friends we share this meal with. Bless them and our family. Amen."

"Amen!" shrieked Rosalie, a sound penetrating enough that it could have substituted for a dog whistle.

Chase winced. The kid had a really high-pitched voice. She had to be headed for an operatic career.

Nicky jumped down from his chair and ran around behind Allison, attempting to snatch a piece of garlic bread off the plate at her elbow.

She snared his hand. "You know the rules, Nicky. If you want to eat, you have to sit in your chair like a big boy and ask to have the bread passed to you."

"No, no, Nicky!" Rosie exclaimed.

The boy made a face at his sister. "You're not the boss of me, Ro-Ro."

Taking Nicky by the shoulders, Allison urged the boy back to his seat as easily as she might have put a mislaid book back on its proper shelf.

Impressed, Chase decided Allison was born to be a mother.

She passed the spaghetti, garlic bread and a bowl of salad around the table. It took a while to get everyone served, including the children. Nicky refused the salad, insisting that was sissy food.

"Where'd you hear that?" Sam asked.

"Bart said so."

"Bart at your school?"

Nicky nodded.

"Well, I've got news for Bart." Sam served his son a small helping of salad with a slice of tomato on top. "All those big kids on my basketball team love salad. It helps them to stay healthy, and grow big and tall. You want to grow up big and tall, don't you?"

Nicky looked skeptical, and Chase noted the boy mostly spread the bits of lettuce around on his plate. In contrast, Chase wolfed down several bites of both salad and spaghetti before even taking a breath.

"This is what I call good home cooking," he said at last. "I haven't had spaghetti this good in ages."

Allison nodded in appreciation of his compliment. "I'm glad you like it."

As they continued to eat, Viv related how at least two dogs had found new homes because of Doggie Daze and Chase's pet adoption day.

"That's great," Sam said.

"It is," Chase agreed. "But Annabelle at the shelter was telling us that they're in serious financial trouble. She and the mayor are trying to come up with a way to raise money to keep it going. With the factory gone and less support from the town, a lot of their funding has vanished."

"We should try to find a way to help them raise more money," Allison said. "Maybe I can talk to the mayor, too. I'm sure everyone in town would want to keep the shelter in business."

"I guess we could pass the hat around town. Or put donation jars on the counters in all the downtown stores. That might generate a few bucks," Chase suggested between bites of spaghetti.

Yeah, but that wouldn't raise much money, Chase realized. The idea would have to be bigger than putting a few dimes and nickels in a couple of jars around town.

When they finished eating, Sam helped clear the table, and Allison served up ice cream and bakery cookies, which seemed to please the children even more than the spaghetti.

As he took his first bite of ice cream, Chase felt a tug on his sleeve.

Rosie said, "Mister, where are you and the lady's kids? Don't they like ice cream?"

A bite of cold ice cream nearly slipped down his windpipe. He coughed. "Uh, we don't have any kids." He turned to Viv to bail him out.

"We aren't married, honey," Viv told Rosie. "So we don't have any children."

The child wore a serious expression as though puzzling over the facts of life. "My daddy and Allison aren't married, but Nicky and me are their kids."

"Yes, well…" Chase said.

"Your daddy and I are going to be married soon, Rosie-Roo," Allison explained. "Vivian and Chase are just dating, like your daddy and I used to date."

Chase's chin snapped up. So did Viv's. *Dating?*

Was this actually a date? Chase wondered. It pretty much seemed that way, he admitted.

Although he wasn't exactly sure about how he felt about that, he reached over to squeeze her hand. A little smile teased around the corners of her lips as she returned the gesture.

Yeah, definitely a date.

When they'd finished dessert, they all pitched in to clear the dishes, then Allison helped the children get ready for bed before she left for home herself. The rest of them settled into the living room, where Chase asked about the upcoming basketball season.

"I think we're in good shape. I've got a kid, Rory Liston, who's got a lot of potential. Assuming he can keep focused on the game."

"He's the youngster who is in Allison's creative writing program, isn't he?" Viv asked.

"Yeah. I thought he could use a little extra attention. I think his home life is pretty shaky these days. He's been letting his grades slip lately."

"I hope he can get his act together." Chase remembered how hard it had been to concentrate in school when his parents fought all the time. The best thing his mom had done was move out and take Chase away from the chaos, even if it had meant she struggled to keep a roof over their heads.

Nicky came racing into the living room wearing pajamas decorated with tiny red and blue airplanes.

He thrust a picture book into Sam's hands. "Read this one!"

Rosie wasn't far behind her brother, presenting a different book to Sam, asserting her preference for bedtime reading in a shrill voice.

With calm dignity, Allison strolled into the living room. "I'm sorry. Reading time has become quite a ritual for the twins."

"I'd say that was appropriate, given you're a bookseller." Viv stood. "Time for us to go, anyway. Dinner was lovely. Thank you for inviting us."

Following Viv's lead, Chase stood. "It was great. Quite a treat for me to have home cooking."

Since Nicky and Rosie had already claimed spots on their dad's lap for reading time, Sam remained seated. Chase walked over to shake his hand, telling him there was no need to get up.

After retrieving their jackets, Allison walked them to the door. "I'll see you at church tomorrow," she said to Viv.

"I'll be there."

Once in the car, Chase leaned back in the seat with a sigh. "Those twins are something else, aren't they?"

"They're adorable, but quite a handful."

Vivian had a smile on her face that suggested she wouldn't mind raising twins. That gave Chase a moment of pause before he pulled away from the curb. He didn't mind being around children, but he didn't intend to raise any himself. Not with the role model he'd had for a father.

No, he wouldn't be responsible for the kind of emotional and physical damage his father had inflicted on him and his mother.

They drove in silence for a couple of blocks, the moonlight flickering through treetops that lined the street. Lights shone in the windows of houses they passed. But they encountered no other cars traveling on their route. Bygones pretty much rolled up the sidewalks after six o'clock, and farmers hit the sack early to be ready to go back to work with the sun.

Bygones definitely didn't offer much nightlife, which was fine with Chase. Apparently that was fine with Viv, as well.

As they approached Viv's house, she said, "Oh, I forgot to tell you what I've decided to do to increase my income."

"I imagine it doesn't have anything to do with cleaning puppy pens."

She laughed. "Please, no. Not that I didn't do my share of cleaning up after the dogs when I lived at home. But I've decided I'm going to write a regular blog about heartland authors and their books. I think I can build it up to the point of getting businesses to post ads on my site."

He glanced over at her. "Hey, that sounds ambitious. And perfect for a book lover like you."

"Yes, I thought so. We'll just have to see if I can put it all together and draw enough followers to make it worthwhile."

"I'm confident you'll make it a success. You've got the skills and the determination."

"Thank you," she whispered. "It means a lot to me that you believe I can succeed."

He pulled into her driveway, and Viv started to get out of the car.

"Hang on a minute," Chase said. "I'll walk you to the door." He went around to the passenger side to help her out.

She hooked her arm through his, and he covered her hand.

"I'm hoping the blog will earn enough that an adoption agency, or a woman who is planning to give up her baby, will see me as a good prospect as an adoptive mom."

Chase jerked to a stop at the foot of the porch steps. "You're going to adopt a baby?"

"I've applied to several adoption agencies."

"But you're single." The shock of her plan had him pointing out the obvious. "It's not easy to be a single parent. That's a lot of responsibility for just one person."

In the porch light, he saw her smooth forehead furrow, and she raised her chin. "I'm aware of that. Which is why I'm trying to increase my income.

I'm also aware that not everyone will approve of my decision to raise a child alone."

He struggled to find something to say that wouldn't upset her further. "I didn't mean to of-fend—"

"Don't worry about it." She released his arm and went up the steps.

Stunned by her revelation, Chase didn't follow her. A few minutes ago he'd been figuring out how he would kiss her good-night on the front porch. Now his head reeled. *Viv? Adopting a baby? Why would she do that?*

She unlocked her door and turned back to him. "It was a lovely evening. Thank you." Her voice sounded tight, her shoulders rigid.

She stepped inside her house, then closed the door behind her and was gone.

Chase stood rooted in place, staring at Essie in the window.

Viv was adopting a baby.

As far as Chase was concerned, that put a kibosh on any deeper relationship with Viv. It was a deal breaker.

With the genes Chase's father had passed down to him, Chase would never risk parenting a child and becoming the abuser his father was. The les-sons he'd learned were too cruel, too heartless a burden for yet another generation of children.

Chapter Six

By the time Vivian heard Chase's car drive away, she was shaking. She sat down hard on the couch. Why had he been so negative about her adopting a baby?

Single women all across the country were enjoying the blessings of motherhood by adopting. She had plenty of emotional support from her family. Her father and brothers would be great male role models for her child.

It couldn't be because Chase hated kids. He obviously enjoyed the youngsters who came to the pet shop to visit the puppies. She'd seen how patient he was with them.

And he'd been fine with the twins tonight, if maybe a little unnerved by Rosie's questions. Of course, Vivian had been, too. And amused.

So why had he so obviously disapproved of her as an adoptive mother?

His reaction had been even more disheartening because they'd been getting along so well. She hadn't wanted the evening to end. She had planned to invite him in for a cup of coffee when he brought her home. But with his attitude about adoption, she'd chucked that plan in a hurry.

And it had hurt.

Essie tiptoed into her lap, circling until she found a comfortable place to curl up.

Vivian stroked her head and smoothed her soft fur.

"What is it with men? I can't have babies, so they dump me as a second-class citizen. And now that I want to adopt, Chase gives me a shocked look like I was planning to steal a child from some poor unsuspecting mother? I just don't get it."

She didn't suppose Essie understood, either, but at least she was a good listener.

She steeled herself against the threat of tears mixed with anger. Her dreams would not be derailed by what a man might or might not support.

No matter how very nice that man might be.

No matter what dreams she might have been harboring about him.

Although she hadn't slept well, Vivian rose the next morning in time to go to church. Since she'd moved from her parents' home to Bygones, she had attended the local church. As a town employee, at the beginning, she'd wanted to be a part of the community. She had found the congregation warm and welcoming, and hadn't regretted her decision.

The white structure stood back from the road, its steeple reaching into a threatening morning sky. The front of the building had a diamond-shaped window and a stately steeple. As she walked toward the entrance, she pulled her jacket more tightly around her. The blustery wind and darkening sky suited her mood. Today she vowed to seek the peace and comfort the Lord provided and try to shake off the distraction of Chase's negative reaction to her plan.

She didn't need his approval to pursue her dreams, she mentally repeated as though it were her mantra.

As was often the case, Mayor Langston was performing the duties of door greeter. He was also the Save Our Streets liaison for Allison and the bookstore.

"Good morning, Vivian." With a warm smile, he handed her a program. The cane he used was hooked over his arm. "How are things going at the bookstore?"

"Very well, I think. We had a special event yesterday that brought in quite a few people." Regretfully, by the end of that evening Vivian had lost the spark of excitement she'd carried throughout most of the day.

"Good to hear it, my dear. We're praying that all our businesses will be profitable for both the owners and our beloved town."

With a nod of acknowledgment, she walked inside the small vestibule and entered the sanctuary. The cloudy day muted the light coming through the stained-glass window as she took a seat on one of the wooden pews. At the front of the church, the pulpit stood to one side, a wooden box with a lectern and microphone on top. Off to the other side, the worship team was playing a prelude.

Bowing her head, Vivian prayed for inner peace and acceptance of God's will, whatever that might be.

Vaguely aware of the church filling with parishioners, she remained in prayer until the worship team struck the notes of the opening hymn, and the sound rang through the church. She stood as Pastor Garman appeared. Tall, slim and balding except for a fringe of light reddish-brown hair, he held up his arms to welcome the congregation.

Despite her best efforts to concentrate on the service, Vivian's mind kept returning to Chase's comments, and the pain they had inflicted. Was it possible she was doing the wrong thing by trying to adopt? She'd taken the question to the Lord more than once. Despite her prayers, she was afraid she wouldn't know His answer until she had exhausted all possibilities to adopt a child.

Meanwhile, she simply had to keep faith that the Lord understood and would grant her the gift of motherhood.

By the time the final hymn was sung, Vivian realized she hadn't achieved the sense of peace that she'd prayed for and was ashamed of her weakness. What other people thought or said about her adopting a baby on her own didn't matter. If the Lord wanted her to have a child to love and raise, then His will would be done.

No one could take that away from her.

As she made her way out of the church, she heard her name called. She turned to find Allison walking toward her.

"Hi, Viv, how are you this morning?"

"I'm fine." She shrugged. "Hope you got the twins to bed all right last night and got yourself home safely."

Her lips twisted into a sheepish grin. "It's always a bit of a struggle. I'm such a pushover when I hear 'Read me another story.' But I do love sticking around to tuck them in for the night."

Vivian gave a knowing laugh. "I'd probably be the same way."

"So how did the drive home with Chase go?"

"Fine." Vivian's gaze slid away, and she focused on a group of children playing on a grassy area in front of the church.

"Uh-oh. Did something happen?"

Vivian sincerely wished Allison wasn't quite so perceptive. "It was nothing, really. I happened to mention that I'd applied to adopt a baby, and Chase went kind of squirrelly on me."

Taking her arm, Allison led her away from the milling crowd. "What do you mean 'squirrelly'?"

She blew out a sigh. "Apparently he doesn't think a single woman should adopt a baby."

"He told you you shouldn't do it?" Allison gasped. "Why, the nerve of him! I would have thought that Chase, of all people, would be very supportive of the idea."

Vivian would have thought so, too. "It doesn't matter," she lied, checking her watch. "I told my mom I'd come to Sunday supper. I'd better get going. I'll see you in the morning."

"Just ignore whatever Chase said. You're going to be a wonderful mom. I feel it right here." She touched her palm to her own chest right over her heart.

"I hope you're right." If and when she had the chance to be a mother.

The clouds had lowered during the service. Now a few drops of rain spattered on the walkway, leaving damp little dots on the concrete. A developing wind rattled the branches on a nearby elm tree, stripping drying leaves that fluttered to the ground.

Allison gave Vivian a quick hug. "Maybe you just misunderstood Chase's reaction."

"I don't think so." As she headed for her car, she spotted Sam coming from the nursery room with the twins. She waved and hurried on. She didn't want to continue her conversation with Allison. Or involve Sam in the topic.

There wasn't any point in rehashing Chase's attitude. He could believe whatever he wanted.

She walked quickly to her car before the rain turned into a downpour.

Vivian's parents owned a full section of land—640 acres—on which they'd grown wheat for as long as she could remember. Recent years had been dry ones, however, and her dad had diversified by raising hogs.

She didn't think her mother was pleased with the change, but Vivian kind of liked the hogs, and the piglets were adorable. Playful little creatures.

She was less pleased when it was time to send them to the slaughterhouse, but the income helped her father to weather the years of drought.

While her car's windshield wipers beat a steady rhythm, Vivian pulled into the long drive and parked near the house. Painted white with dark green trim, the house was a hodgepodge of additions built on over the years to serve their growing family.

Her brother Danny's pickup truck was parked right in front of her. He worked in Wichita as an aircraft technician and usually came to Sunday supper. His twin, David, a college agriculture graduate, worked on a cattle ranch farther east and didn't always make it.

Sophie, a high school senior, and Jake, who was in middle school, still lived at home.

Vivian's big sister Lisa was married, had a cute-as-a-princess three-year-old and lived in Chicago. She and Vivian had been close growing up, and Vivian still missed her. She was glad Lisa would be coming down for Thanksgiving.

Grabbing her purse, Vivian got out of the car and hurried through the rain up onto the wide porch. Being with her family always lifted her spirits, something she needed today.

"Hey, Dad. Danny." The two of them were ensconced on the plaid couch in the living room watching a pro football game on a fifty-inch TV, their typical Sunday afternoon activity in the fall. Little brother Jake lay sprawled on the floor playing some sort of a handheld electronic game. Vivian bent down to kiss her father's cheek.

"Hey, Vivi girl. It's still wet out there, huh?"

"Afraid so." She tossed a smile at Danny. "How many oscilloscopes did you burn up at work last week?"

Dark haired and wiry like their father, Danny scowled at her. "One time. Years ago. And you've been raggin' on me ever since."

"Just my way of checking up on the welfare of our nation's airlines." Since Jake hadn't even bothered to look up when she arrived, she reached down and tickled the twelve-year-old. Which he hated.

He rolled away. "Cut that out!"

"Then say hello to your beloved big sister," she challenged.

"'lo," he grunted, resuming his position on the carpet.

Shedding her coat, she asked, "Where's Mom?"

"In the kitchen." Her dad tilted his head in that direction. "Sophie's helping her with supper."

"I'll go lend a hand." She hung her coat on a coatrack in the hallway and went into the kitchen. The aroma of roasted chicken and biscuits heating in the oven signified home to Vivian. She and her sisters had all spent a lot of time in the kitchen, helping their mother and unburdening their hearts when they were troubled.

"Everything smells wonderful, Mom." She kissed her mother, whose dark brown hair was just beginning to show some gray, and gave Sophie a quick hug. "What can I do to help?"

"Sophie's about to mash the potatoes, but you can set the table, if you'd like."

"Will do." From the sideboard in the dining room, she retrieved the good silver, which was saved for Sunday suppers and holidays. With only six for dinner, extra leaves hadn't been added to the rosewood table, a wedding gift from Grandpa and Grandma Duncan, who had farmed the land since before Vivian's father was born.

The ebb and flow of dinner preparations, the arrival of dishes of steaming homegrown beans and mashed potatoes on the table, and the clink of brightly polished silverware provided a comforting rhythm. Only occasionally was the smooth passage of food to the table broken by a shout or groan from the menfolk watching the football game.

When dinner was called, the TV immediately went off and the football fans trekked in to be seated at the table. They all held hands as Vivian's father said grace.

With her head bowed, Vivian listened to her father's strong voice, and his words touched her heart. Living alone might be practical and closer to her job, but sometimes she was lonely and longed for a loving family of her own like the one her parents had nurtured.

"So, how are plans coming for the church bazaar?" Vivian asked her mother, who was chairing the event this year.

"Fine, I think. Bette Sue has talked with all the craft groups in the area, inviting them to bring their merchandise to sell. Arnetta is lining up people to bring baked goods."

"Mindy's planning to bake a couple of cakes and

leave one home for us, aren't you, sweetheart?" Vivian's father rubbed his tummy enthusiastically.

"I always do, don't I, dear," she answered with a fond smile. "I'll have two afghans ready for the bazaar, too."

It always impressed Vivian how creative her mother was with a needle and thread or yarn, and how few of those genes she had inherited.

During the rest of the dinner, conversation flowed concerning school and jobs, and the ever-present topic of the weather.

Since Sophie had helped with dinner preparations, Vivian volunteered to help with cleanup.

She rinsed the dinner plates and put them in the dishwasher while her mother stored leftovers in the refrigerator.

"You were quiet during dinner," her mother said. "Is anything wrong?"

Mom could always see through her moods. "Not really. But I did get a letter from one of the adoption agencies rejecting me."

"Oh, I'm so sorry, dear."

"It will be all right. They didn't think I earned enough to support a child, so I figured out how I can make more money." She explained about the book blog she intended to write and how it would take her a while to build up the business.

"You'll find a way to make it happen. I know you will. You've always been such a determined child."

Vivian laughed. "I'm not quite sure whether that's good or bad."

"I've always known the Lord had something special in mind for you." Her mother gave her a quick hug. "You simply have to have faith He knows what He's doing, and let Him lead you on the path He intends for you."

That sounded so simple. In practice, trying to determine what God had in mind was fraught with false steps and potholes. Sometimes those false steps could hurt. A lot.

She squeezed her eyes shut. *Let go, let God.* That's what she'd have to do and then pray that she'd make the right decisions.

By Monday morning, Chase knew he had to apologize to Viv. He'd had no right to tell her that she shouldn't become a single mom if that's what she wanted.

He fed the puppies and kittens, and cleaned their pens, keeping an eye out for Viv's arrival at the bookstore. He'd been a jerk Saturday night. Granted, he wasn't cut out to be a father. That would be too big a risk considering his father's abysmal record as a parent. He had read plenty of books and articles about how abusive parenting was passed on down to children. The kind of thing Chase had learned at the end of his father's fist.

A flash of forgotten memory came back to him, sharp and painful.

He'd come across a snapshot of his father when his dad was about ten, Chase's age at the time. The two of them had looked the same—dark black hair, brown eyes squinting into the sun and lips that rarely smiled.

If Chase had inherited those traits from his father, he could just as well have ended up with an abusive one.

Later he'd asked his mother about that. She'd denied the possibility. Chase hadn't believed her.

He still didn't. Still too afraid to trust his mother's word.

Unconsciously, he rubbed the scar on his chin. With Viv so determined to adopt, it meant they couldn't have a future together.

But they could still be friends. Colleagues. Fellow residents of Bygones. He hadn't meant to hurt her feelings.

Standing at the front counter, he peered out the window. Waiting. His chest hurt and his neck muscles were as taut as a Rottweiler straining at his leash.

The rain had kept up most of yesterday, and the clouds were still misting the bricks of Main Street, making them shiny and reflecting the streetlights that were still on.

"Poor baby. Poor baby." Pepper ducked his head under his wing and made a cooing sound.

"I appreciate your sympathy, but it's my own fault. Sticking my nose into somebody else's business." He offered a grape to Pepper, who snapped it from Chase's fingers and hopped up on the perch to enjoy the tidbit.

Viv's car went by and angled into a parking place.

Taking a deep breath, Chase grabbed his jacket and went out the door. The cold, damp air sent a chill through him. He hugged the storefronts, staying under the protective awnings until he reached the bookstore.

Viv opened her car door, climbed out and spotted him. She stood stock-still for a moment. She wore a floppy pink rain hat and a khaki raincoat, her expression unreadable.

"Hi," he said. "Not very good weather, is it?"

"Except during harvesting, farmers are happy whenever it rains."

Yeah, Chase supposed that was true. "Have you got a minute?"

"Sure." The word carried as much enthusiasm as a flat tire.

He waited while she unlocked the door and stepped inside. As she flicked the lights on, he followed her in, closing the door behind him.

Tugging her hat off, she turned toward him. "Is there a problem?"

"If there is, it's me who has the problem. I came to apologize for what I said Saturday night."

A tiny frown marred her smooth forehead. "You don't owe me an apology."

"I think I do. At least I need to tell you why I was rude when you said you were going to adopt a baby."

She gave a quiet nod. "All right."

"You see…" He had to clear the tightness of memories from his throat. "I told you the other day that I was raised by a single mother. It was really tough going. For both of us. She worked two jobs just to keep a roof over our heads and food on the table. We had to move around a lot." He couldn't remember how many times they'd been evicted because his mother hadn't had the money to pay the rent. "When you told me what you had in mind, my first reaction was that I didn't want you to go through what my mother had. I'm sorry for how I acted."

Her expression softened. A little smile tugged at her lips. "It's all right, Chase. I'm glad you told me." She reached out her hand as though she wanted to touch his cheek, but then dropped it away.

"Yeah, well, I guess single parenthood is a hot-button issue with me," he said.

"After your experience, I can understand that."

"I hope so." Instinctively, Chase rubbed at the scar on his chin. Being evicted hadn't been the worst of his experiences. The situation had been far rougher when he and his mother had still been living with his father.

Vivian set her rain hat on the counter and shrugged out of her raincoat. "Do you want some coffee?"

He did, but he didn't think he should linger. He didn't want to mislead her about their future. "Not today. I've got some paperwork to do this morning."

The lie tasted as bitter as day-old coffee on his tongue as he stepped out of the bookshop to return to Fluff & Stuff. Viv deserved so much more than he could ever give her.

Just as Chase was leaving, Vivian heard Allison come in the back door. With her coat still draped over her arm, Vivian went into the back room to hang it up.

Allison was doing the same with her jacket. "Did I hear Chase out front?"

"He just left." She reached for a hanger.

Allison's eyebrows rose. "I thought you were mad at him."

"I wasn't *mad* at him. I was a bit hurt and disappointed. But he explained why he'd reacted the way he did." Not many men would apologize for what had been simply their opinion based on their personal experience. It had warmed her heart to think he cared that much about her feelings.

"So what did he say?"

"He'd already told me he'd been raised by a single mother, and he said how hard it had been for her. Apparently, his first reaction was that he didn't want me to go through that, too."

"That's sweet." Allison got her jacket hung up and took Vivian's raincoat, hanging it next to her own. "Explaining himself was a lovely thing to do. I'd hate to think we'd have a feud going on between our two shops."

"I don't think that would ever happen." At heart, Vivian sensed Chase was too good a man to hold a grudge or be cruel in any way. "All of us in Bygones want the same thing—for the town and the businesses to survive and thrive." Regret nipped at her that a business relationship with Chase was all that she would ever have.

With a mental sigh, she set to work reshelving misplaced books and straightening stock.

After a quiet hour or so, Mayor Langston walked into the bookshop. His cane tapped lightly on the floor with each step he took. A brown hat spotted with raindrops covered his thinning gray hair.

"Good morning, ladies," he said, tipping his hat. "A lovely Kansas day, isn't it?"

"If you're a farmer," Allison countered. "Not quite so good if you're a bookseller. You're the first person to cross our threshold this morning."

"Then I feel especially welcome. I meant to catch

you after church yesterday, Allison. Wanted to remind you that the meeting for the new shopkeepers is tomorrow night at the coffee shop."

"That's right! I have something I want to propose to the group. I've been talking to a direct mail delivery business. It seems to me with Christmas coming, we should combine our resources to send flyers to the residents of neighboring towns. While a lot of people buy books online, there's nothing better than browsing the shelves in an actual bookstore to come up with gift ideas. We're the only bookstore between Junction City and Wichita. I imagine Melissa's bakery is the only one around, too, as well as Lily's flower shop."

The mayor lifted his cane in approval. "An excellent idea. Be sure to bring that up at the meeting."

"I will. It also occurs to me that Lily should be back in her flower shop today. I'll have to pop over to hear about her honeymoon."

Vivian smiled. "I'm sure they had a wonderful time. She and Tate seem perfect for each other."

"Indeed," the mayor said, turning to Vivian. "On Sunday I spoke to Annabelle from the shelter. She was very impressed with the way you and Chase worked so well together for your Doggie Daze event."

Her cheeks warmed. "Thank you. That was Allison's idea, of course. We just carried it out."

"I understand. But nonetheless, it went well, and

Annabelle and I would like to impose on you and Chase to help out the shelter even more directly."

A skitter of nerves sped down Vivian's spine. "Of course. I'd be happy to help in any way I can." Although given Chase's view of a single mother adopting a child, Vivian wasn't so sure they'd make a grand team together anymore.

"I also happened to pop into the library to see Mrs. Peacock," he said. "She told me you had helped her organize a read-a-thon for the youngsters in town."

"Yes, that's true." Vivian had no idea where the mayor was going with this.

"It seems our animal shelter is in dire need of financial support. Both Annabelle and Mrs. Peacock suggested you and Chase could put such a fundraising project together and make a success of it. As a special favor to our little town."

"What a wonderful idea!" Allison piped up.

Vivian's gaze snapped from the mayor to Allison and back again. She swallowed hard. "Have you, um, talked to Chase about this yet?" What if he didn't want to work with her? Even though she knew the shelter was important to him, working with her might not be his idea of a good match.

"Not yet, m'dear. But I do plan to speak to him soon."

"I see. Well, then…" She left the thought dangling on a wisp of hope…or fear of what his answer might be.

"Assuming Chase agrees to help out, I'll the leave the details of the read-a-thon up to you two." He touched the brim of his hat. "Thank you, ladies. I'll be off now. I'm confident Bygones will survive these trying times because of good people like you."

With a jaunty flip of his cane, the mayor went out the door.

Vivian's mouth was stuck open like a fly trap.

"The read-a-thon is a great idea, Viv. I'm glad the mayor thought of it."

Slowly, Vivian turned back to Allison. "It may be a good idea. But I'm not all that sure Chase will want to work with me on the project."

A smile that spoke of love and caring curved Allison's lips. "Viv, Chase is going to love working with you. Don't you doubt that for a minute."

Vivian couldn't help but question Allison's opinion. It had been clear later Saturday night, and again this morning, that Chase wanted to keep their relationship as distant as possible.

It seemed as though Chase was barely back from seeing Viv when Mayor Langston showed up in his shop.

Pepper greeted the mayor with a shrill, "Pretty birdie!"

"Good morning, Mayor." Chase set aside the bag

of cat food he had been about to shelve and walked to the front of the store.

The mayor extended his hand. "How are things going for you these days?" Despite his age, his grip was sure and firm.

"Business is good and picking up, I'd say."

"Excellent." The mayor glanced around the store and nodded with approval. "I have a project I'd like you to help with, if you think you have time."

Given that Mayor Langston was an influential man around town, Chase wasn't in any position to turn him down. Besides, Chase liked being a part of this community. "Sure. What do you need?"

"Annabelle and I have come up with a scheme to raise money for the shelter. She tells me you're very supportive, so you were at the top of my list to help coordinate the project."

Chase felt an uneasy tightening creep along his nape. "Just what kind of a project are we talking about?"

"A read-a-thon."

Pepper jiggled his string of silver bells and squawked.

Chase blinked. "A read-a-who?"

"It's a bit like those 5K and 10K walks folks do for fund-raising, except instead of walking so many miles, they read a bunch of books. People pledge to contribute so many dollars per book read, and the money goes to the nonprofit which is sponsoring the event. In this case, the animal shelter."

"O...kay." He dragged out the word. "But I'm not sure I'm the best person to organize that kind of a project. Maybe Mrs. Peacock at the library?"

"Actually, Mrs. Peacock recommended Vivian at the bookstore. Viv ran a similar project for the library and said she'd be delighted to help out with this."

"Vivian." Her name slipped out in a whisper. "You're saying she and I are going to—"

"Work together." The mayor seemed quite pleased with that decision. "You know all about the shelter. She's got experience running a read-a-thon. A perfect match."

Chase didn't agree with that at all. In fact, his goal was to avoid a close, even professional, relationship with Viv. He needed distance from Viv. Needed to stay away from temptation. Needed to keep his head on straight and remember she wanted to adopt a baby.

Chase couldn't be any part of that.

The mayor tilted his head. "Is that a problem? Working with Vivian, I mean? Because Bygones has already lost so much, we can't lose our animal shelter, too. Hard times or not, we have to save some of the goodness that is part of our town."

Swallowing hard, Chase nodded. The town had already given him a second chance at a new life. How could he tell the mayor no? *Sorry, Your Honor. I don't dare work with Viv on anything because that might lead to getting close to her and maybe even falling for her. And that would be the worst thing that could ever happen to her...and the baby she wants to adopt.*

He cleared his throat. "No, there's no problem with Viv and me working together." He'd simply have to watch himself. Stay in control. Think of her as a business associate. *No problem.*

The mayor's smile was so broad; it was nothing but shiny white teeth. "Excellent. Then I'll count on you two to get together soon. Perhaps you can start tomorrow evening at the shopkeepers' meeting."

A knife twisted in Chase's back. "We'll get on it right away."

"Of course, unless you can think of a better idea to raise money for the shelter...."

"No, no. The read-a-thon ought to work." Assuming Viv knew what she was doing, because he sure didn't.

As soon as the mayor left, Chase picked up the phone. He didn't have to meet with Viv in person to schedule a time to start planning the read-a-thon. In fact, talking on the phone was a far better way to go than face-to-face.

Chapter Seven

Tuesday evening, right after he had closed up the shop, Chase strolled over to the Cozy Cup Café for the shopkeepers' meeting.

Josh Smith, the owner of the café, was behind the counter playing barista for Coraline Connolly, the unofficial chairperson of the Save Our Streets committee. With her strong yet warm personality, Coraline had been a fine leader for the SOS committee. If anyone could lead Bygones back to prosperity, Coraline's faith and heart could do it.

"Good evening, Chase." Josh sent him a casual wave. A quiet guy, he rarely said anything during their meetings. "Can I fix you a cappuccino? Or maybe a peppermint mocha frappuccino? That's our flavor of the month."

"Sounds a little too rich for me. How 'bout a straight cappuccino with decaf?"

"Coming right up." Josh handed Coraline her

drink. She carried it to the small round wrought-iron table where Dale Eversleigh was already seated. In his forties, Dale was a third-generation undertaker and operated the Eversleigh Funeral Home in Bygones.

Chase strolled over to Dale. "You're here early. Business must be slow in town these days."

Dale looked up with a slight smile. "Generally that's a good thing for a town, fewer people dying. In our case it means so many people have moved away, somebody else is going to get their business."

"Guess that would be a problem," Chase agreed.

"Same thing with my students," Coraline said. "Seems like every day a youngster or two drops out and moves away."

"Well, let's hope business on Main Street picks up enough to bring some of them back to town."

"Chase!" Josh called to him and held up Chase's cappuccino.

He went to the counter to pick it up. "Thanks."

"You're welcome." Immediately Josh turned back to the cappuccino machine to make the next order.

In addition to the coffee business, Josh had divided the shop with a low partition to set off one side of the space for computer stations. Chase had noticed a fair number of teenagers took advantage of the setup. Most of them were boys with, infrequently, a teenage girl tagging along. The computer games Josh had installed were apparently all the rage.

Tate and Lily Bronson, the newlyweds, came in the door followed closely by Melissa Sweeney from the bakery. Everyone took the opportunity to applaud and call out to the bride and groom again, making Lily blush. Coraline was first on her feet to give Lily a hug.

Chase hung back, keeping his eye on the door as the owner of the hardware store, Patrick Fogerty, came in with Joe Sheridan, the chief of police.

Although they'd talked on the phone to set up a read-a-thon meeting for tomorrow morning, Chase hadn't seen Viv since early yesterday morning. Wanting to see her itched at him like a burr under his skin. A burr he didn't dare scratch.

Josh kept the cappuccino machine roaring as other committee members arrived. But still no Allison. Or Viv.

Chase picked a table off to the side and sat down to enjoy his cappuccino.

Coraline took the floor. "I think most of us are here."

Just then the door opened to admit Allison, Viv right behind her. Chase's breath caught. He wanted to stand. To offer Viv the chair next to his. But he held his ground. Surely she'd sit with Allison.

"Sorry we're late," Allison said to no one in particular. "Some customers have to read the whole book before deciding to buy it." That got a chuckle from the group, and she sat with the police chief.

Looking as chipper as if she'd just started her day, Viv glanced around and eyed the empty chair at Chase's table. "Is that seat taken?"

"No, no." He popped to his feet. "Help yourself."

A faint smile, one that didn't reach her eyes, lifted her lips. "Thanks." She slid in next to him.

"You want Josh to make you a drink?" he asked in a whisper.

"No, I'm fine. Thanks. How was your day?"

"I sold a couple of jackets for a Pomeranian. Her owner figured it was going to be a cold winter. And I got a call about Pepper."

Her eyes widened, making them shine a dark blue in the overhead lights. "Someone wants to buy him?"

"It sounded like a decent bite. We'll see."

Viv's frown suggested she wasn't pleased with the idea. "You're going to miss him when he's gone."

"Maybe. Kind of like missing a sore tooth." That wasn't quite true. The bird was beginning to grow on him. A bit like a wart in some ways, but he did get a kick out of the way Pepper greeted his customers. Even though Pepper sometimes insulted them, they didn't seem to mind.

Vivian turned toward Coraline, who had started

the meeting, leaving Chase feeling as though a cool breeze had washed over him. *One smart lady.*

"I specifically asked Chief Sheridan to give us an update tonight on the vandalism that's been going on around town. So do you have any suspects? Or even better, have you caught anyone yet?" Coraline asked.

Sheridan stood, his back ramrod straight as though he was still a member of the Marine Corps. "Not yet, I'm afraid. Whoever is the culprit, he's pretty sneaky. We haven't had a single sighting."

Chase spoke up. "Did you hear about Amos Mahnken having his cows get loose because someone pulled down his fence? He lives just outside the town limits near Highway 135."

Turning toward Chase, the chief shook his head. "Nope. Didn't hear about that. It's not my jurisdiction."

"I'll tell you about it after the meeting." Chase realized he probably should have reported the incident at the time. But he'd been so dazzled by Viv that he hadn't even thought about it.

Conscious of Viv sitting close him, and trying to mentally block the enticing scent of her shampoo, Chase listened halfheartedly to the general discussion about the vandalism and the shopkeepers' concerns.

Sheridan pleaded that he simply didn't have enough officers left to spend much time tracking down the culprit. Other crimes had a higher priority. That resulted in a fair amount of grumbling from the SOS committee members and the merchants.

The door opened again and Robert Randall, the owner of the factory that had closed in town, stepped inside. Dressed casually in chinos and a windbreaker, he looked like a man of leisure.

"Robert!" Coraline's eyes lit up, and she greeted the man with a big smile. "I'm so glad you could come this evening."

"You know I always come when you call." His lips quirked into a subtle smile as he strolled toward her. His easy gait and relaxed air belied his past as a corporate CEO and all the stress he'd experienced by closing the factory.

Chase knew initially Randall wasn't convinced the new shops would bring in enough money and taxes to make it worthwhile for the town or fill its coffers. But as the shopkeepers had reported increasing success, Randall seemed to have gotten on board with the project and mellowed about the town's future.

"Do tell everyone about the phone call you received," Coraline requested.

"As I explained to you, there isn't a whole lot to tell. Nothing to get excited about," he insisted.

Coraline touched his arm. "There could be, Robert. Just tell them."

He shook his head in denial. "A man called me. He didn't identify himself. He asked a lot of basic questions about the factory. Square footage. What machinery was still in the building. What repairs, if any, would be needed if a party was interested in reopening the plant."

"Did he want to buy the place?" Mayor Langston asked.

Chief Sheridan asked, "Did you recognize his voice?"

Under her breath, Viv said, "Some people in town think Coraline herself is the benefactor."

Chase's brows shot up. "Really?" He hadn't considered that at all. In the first place, how would a schoolteacher turned principal have the kind of money the benefactor had invested in Bygones?

Randall held up his hand for silence. "Like I said, no reason to get excited. He didn't say anything about buying the place. And, no, I didn't recognize his voice, although he sounded familiar." He shrugged. "It's always hard to identify voices over the phone."

Viv shot Chase a quick look. "Wouldn't it be wonderful if the factory reopened?" she whispered. "All those people who were laid off could come back to work."

"Randall said we shouldn't get our hopes up," Chase responded.

"Sometimes hope is all we have," Viv said.

For much of Chase's life, hope had been in short supply.

Coraline hooked her arm through Randall's. "From what you've said, Robert, it doesn't sound like a random call to me."

"Could've been a Realtor, for all I know," he countered.

"A Realtor would have introduced himself," Coraline insisted. "I am confident that with all the work we've done to build the town back up, something wonderful is going to happen. Maybe this man who called you is the person who will propel the town back into true prosperity."

"You're the most optimistic person I know," Randall said, his tone both admiring and affectionate.

"That's because I have faith in the Lord and His good works." She gave him a friendly push. "Go sit down and hear what else these wonderful people have in mind for our community."

While Coraline might be an optimist, Chase had to rate Viv pretty high on that scale, too. A single woman deciding to adopt a child all on her own? That was either optimism or sheer foolishness. Chase didn't think Viv had a foolish bone in her very attractive body.

But maybe she didn't fully understand how difficult it was to be a single mom. His mother had learned that lesson. The hard way.

A bit later, when the topic of the unknown caller had calmed down, Allison stood to explain an idea she had.

"Christmas is almost upon us," she said. "I'm going to suggest that we all combine our resources and produce an insert for the *Bygones Gazette* and as something to circulate in surrounding towns to encourage people to shop for Christmas here in Bygones."

The mayor spoke up. "Allison mentioned this idea to me. I think it's a good one."

"We could include a discount coupon of some sort that could be used in any of our stores," Allison continued.

"I could go for that," Chase said. "Ten or fifteen percent off everything except pet food would encourage people to shop locally."

"Right," Elwood Dill agreed. "Maybe I could get rid of some of that old junk my wife won't let me throw out."

Everyone laughed, knowing full well Elwood was a born hoarder and would give up some of his most precious possessions only under great duress.

The committee members agreed that Allison would be the point person for creating the ad, and that each business would be responsible for providing her with the information she needed.

A few minutes later, the meeting broke up. Chase was tempted to walk Viv to her car, but he'd promised the sheriff he'd tell him about the incident at Amos's place. Just as well. If he was going to keep his distance from Viv, he should start now.

"I'll see you right here in the morning," he said to Viv.

"I'll be here bright and early."

He suppressed a groan. Nothing about keeping away from Viv was going to be easy.

Vivian checked her watch as she parked in front of the Cozy Cup Café the next morning. *Late!* Despite the futility of her hope for a relationship with Chase, she'd been excited about meeting him for coffee, and then she'd been delayed. By Roger!

Laptop in hand, she rushed up to the café door. It opened just as she reached for the handle.

Chase greeted her with a bland expression, his brown eyes somehow troubled. "Good morning."

"I'm so sorry I'm late." A little breathless and deflated by his unenthusiastic greeting, she slipped past him into the warmth of the café. "It was all the fault of that silly hamster you sold me."

"Roger's fault?" He cocked his head. "What did he do?"

She shed her jacket with Chase's help. Beneath that she wore a soft sweater and a wool skirt, a comfortable yet attractive outfit she thought she looked good in.

"I was putting fresh food in his dish and he es

caped. Jumped right out the cage. He literally flew off the desk. I thought he had killed himself." She spoke so rapidly she could hardly catch her breath. "He ran way back under the desk and hid when I screamed." Vivian had been terrified she'd lose the creature, that he would somehow sneak outside and become breakfast for a passing hawk.

"But he was okay?"

"After I finally lured him out from under the desk with a big ol' carrot, he was fine. Greedy little guy."

Chuckling, Chase held out a chair for her at one of the round tables. "I'm sure he enjoyed his adventure."

"Well, you can be sure I won't give him another chance to escape. And if I do, I'll…I'll leave him for Essie to take care of."

Chase barked a laugh that came from deep in his chest. The spark in his eyes erased the earlier worry she'd seen and drew Vivian, causing her heart rate to slow to a heavy beat.

Sitting down, Vivian immediately reached for the cup of coffee already at her place.

"If it's cold, I'll get you a fresh cup. Josh just stepped into the back room."

She sipped the coffee and nodded. "It's fine. And the pastry looks yummy. Thanks." With a sigh, she broke off a bite and tucked it in her mouth, enjoying the rich buttery flavor. "So, about the read-a-thon.

How do you think we ought to run and promote it to raise the most money for the shelter?"

"Truth is, I never even heard of a read-a-thon until the mayor talked to me about it yesterday. Why don't you explain what this is all about?"

"Sure." She broke off another bit of roll. "At the library, during the summer, we had a read-a-thon for the kids. The more books they read, the more prizes they got. Nothing big—things like pencils and spiral notebooks. But some of the youngsters really got into it."

"How does that help the shelter?" Chase asked. "We want to raise money, not give away stuff that costs us money."

"I know." She turned in her chair to face him more directly. "This time we'll run it like they do walkathons for charities. People get pledges from family and friends for every mile they walk, and all the money goes to a good cause."

"Oh, yeah, the mayor said something about a walkathon."

"We could set it up so that it didn't matter where people get their books to read. They won't have to buy them." Viv felt invigorated, the thoughts coming out almost as quickly as she could say the words. "I can talk to Mrs. Peacock at the library. We could run the read-a-thon in conjunction with her. And I'm sure Mrs. Connolly at the school would help out. They must have library books available for the kids, too."

"Sounds good to me. At least you know what you're talking about, which is more than I do."

"Don't worry." She reached out to touch his arm, but in a subtle gesture, he pulled back. Her lower lip trembled. She pulled it between her teeth. Why in the world was he so afraid to let her touch him? Let her care about him?

"Since you have the contact with the shelter," she continued, trying not to let the hurt show, "you can handle that end of things. Maybe we can get Whitney to write another article and feature pictures of a dog or two and a couple of cats that are available. We can call it the Happy Tales Read-a-thon."

"I like the sound of that. I'll talk with Whitney and coordinate with Annabelle at the shelter."

"That would help a lot." She mentally went through all the steps that needed to be done to make the read-a-thon a success. "How do you feel about being treasurer?"

"Me?" He lifted his shoulders in an easy shrug. "That shouldn't be too hard. I'd have to open a bank account. We'd need two signatures for withdrawals to be sure the funds are all used for the shelter. I can arrange that at the bank tomorrow."

"Good idea. Will it work to have the kids turn in their pledges and checks to us at Happy Endings, and then we'll turn them over to you for deposit?"

He thought for a minute. "Sure, that's okay. We'll need to make copies of all the checks we receive before I deposit them and give receipts for cash so there's a record of what we take in."

It pleased Vivian to know how careful Chase would be with the money they raised for the shelter. In addition to being good-looking, kind and generous, he was also an honest man, she thought with an inner grin.

Matt Garman, a teenager, strolled in the front door. Chase looked up and greeted him. "Hey, Matt. Aren't you supposed to be in school at this time of day?"

"I gotta drop off my grandpa's laptop. I think he's got a virus. Josh said he'd take a look, see if he could fix it."

"Do you think Mrs. Connolly will accept that excuse for being late?" Vivian asked. The lanky young man worked part-time for Josh and lived with his grandfather, Pastor Garman, while his father served as a missionary overseas. A friendly kid, he was hardworking and good with customers.

His youthful cheeks flushed. "I told my first-period instructor I'd be late."

"Good for you." Vivian had a spark of inspiration. "Say, Matt, we're putting together a read-a-thon to raise money for Happy Havens Animal

Shelter. Do you think high school students would be interested in participating?"

"I dunno." As Josh came out from the back room, Matt put his grandfather's laptop on the counter. He turned back to Vivian. "Sounds like a good idea to me. I can sort of ask around, if you want."

"That would be great. I'll take some entry forms out to Ms. Connolly tomorrow or the next day. Maybe you can stir up some interest."

"The way to get the attention of kids these days," Josh said, "is to spread the word on YouTube and Facebook and Twitter. Kids don't talk to each other. They tweet."

"You have that right," Chase said. "I had a buddy set up a Facebook page and a website for Fluff & Stuff."

Matt checked with Josh then returned his attention to Vivian. "I could maybe do something like that. I'd need more information though."

"We're calling it Happy Tales Read-a-thon. If you'll give me your email address, I'll send you the form I'm putting together." Excited about the prospect of some internet exposure, Vivian jotted down the boy's address, promising to send him the information in the next day or two.

Opening her laptop, Vivian slanted it so Chase could see the entry form she'd been working on. On a background of silhouetted dogs and cats, she had described the need to raise money and left space for the child's name plus lines to list pledges. On the back of the form, the youngsters were to list the titles of the books they had read.

Her hand brushed against Chase's arm as they leaned close together, his soft sweater a caress on her skin. A simmering warmth stole through her. She didn't pull away. Instead she cherished the sensation, wanting it to last, and knowing it wouldn't.

She jerked away when Matt finished his business with Josh, told them "So long," and hurried off to school. He'd return after his classes to help out at the café.

Taking a deep breath, Vivian refocused her attention on the computer screen. "Should we set a goal for the read-a-thon? How much money we want to raise?"

"I imagine they'll be happy with whatever they get," Chase said.

Josh strolled over to their table. "I'd go bigger than that. Set the goal for the shelter's annual budget. If you don't let people know how much they really need, then you'll be nickeled and dimed, and won't raise nearly enough to do any good."

Vivian swallowed hard. She hadn't anticipated setting such an ambitious goal, but it did make sense.

"I like that idea," Chase agreed. "I'll check with Annabelle about the budget."

"Matt's a pretty sharp kid," Josh said. "I'll help him put something up on the internet that will draw attention to the read-a-thon."

"Maybe we could use one of those cardboard thermometers with a red line showing how close we're getting to the goal," Chase suggested.

Thrilled by all the great ideas, Vivian said, "Perfect. We could put the thermometer in Happy Endings's front window so everyone in town can keep track. We can publicize the website address that Matt sets up, too. This is going to be—"

"Awesome," Chase said with pride in his voice.

A husky purr of pleasure filled her chest at how well they worked together. Even so, she knew Chase's reaction to her adoption plan had already severed the tenuous romantic connection between them she'd felt. Perhaps severed it beyond repair.

But they were still friends, for which she was grateful.

Shortly before noon, Chase popped his head into the bookshop. "You busy?" he asked Vivian.

Holding an armful of books she was shelving, she shook her head. "Not really."

"Good." He stepped inside and closed the door behind him. "I talked with Annabelle. The shelter was running on an annual budget of ten thousand dollars when the town was funding it. If they had any paid staff, it would be a lot higher than that.

Now they're down to maybe two thousand dollars in contributions."

"Oh, dear. No wonder they're considering closing the shelter. But do you think we can raise the whole ten thousand with the read-a-thon?" Her heart sank. She had hoped to raise a thousand or two. Definitely not ten.

"Hey, you're the optimist around here. The one with all the faith."

Her forehead tightened into a frown. "I may have faith in God, but it's a little scary to go to Him for help with an impossible request."

"Josh thought we should set our target high. So I guess we won't know if it's impossible unless we ask." He winked at her. "Gotta get back to the shop. We'll talk more later."

The door closed behind him.

Books still in her arms, Vivian stood there thinking. Maybe Chase was right. It couldn't hurt to ask.

Well, Lord, what do You think? Is ten thousand too much to ask for? The dogs and cats in the shelter could sure use Your help. I'll be happy to do my part and let You guide me if You think it's a good idea.

Anxious to learn what the Lord's answer to her prayer would be, Vivian shifted her attention back to shelving the books. She was already keeping

the Lord busy with her prayers for a baby to adopt.
Maybe she was asking for too much.

Only time would tell.

Chapter Eight

As soon as her boss had approved the Happy Tales Read-a-thon entry form, Vivian emailed it to Matt Garman, along with the information about how much money they hoped to raise. She also gave him the bookstore's phone and her cell number in case he had questions.

Then she printed a batch of forms to deliver to the shops in town, the library and the school.

"If this keeps up, I'm going to open my own delivery service," she said to Allison.

"I'm sure you'd be a smashing success, but if our mail carrier can't compete with you, we wouldn't want Bea to lose her job. Or undermine her weight-loss program," Allison said, laughing.

Beatrice Jorgensen, known as Bea, had applied for the job nearly ten years ago, hoping all the walking would help her to lose weight. So far it hadn't worked. But she certainly could outwalk anyone else in town, and rain or snow never slowed her down.

"By the way," Allison said. "Instead of bothering to make up one of those thermometers you wanted to put in the window, I ordered one from a distributor. They're not expensive. We'll probably get it by Saturday, or at the latest, Monday."

"Good. By then we'll have these entry forms all over town. And I'll give Chase a batch to take to the shelter."

"You know what? I'm going to call those folks back and order a second thermometer for the shelter. Seems to me everyone who goes to the shelter to pick out a pet, or leave one, would be a potential donor."

"You're absolutely right." Vivian admired Allison for her business sense as well as for her commitment to the community. "I do want to coordinate with Mrs. Peacock at the library, though. I think I'll go there first. This is one of the few afternoons the library is open." The library was a major victim of the cutbacks the town had had to make and the reason Vivian had lost her job there.

Gathering up a handful of forms, she left the bookshop and walked to Bronson Park, which was located at the edge of town. Named for the founders of Bygones, Saul and Paul Bronson, the park included an irregularly shaped pond, a lovely stopover for migrating ducks as well as those who stayed in residence year-round. Several ducks cruised along the rippling surface of the water, from time to time dipping their heads to bob for food on the shallow bottom.

There was also a playground and gazebo. With a cold November breeze blowing, the park was empty. Only a few leaves and bits of paper scampered across the grassy area.

Vivian tugged her jacket more tightly around her and headed for the boxy two-story stone building that was the original homestead of Saul Bronson, which now housed the town library.

Inside, she inhaled the scent of old books, glue and printers' ink, and relished the warmth the aging heating system had managed to produce. Nostalgia swept over her. She loved libraries and everything about them. And she missed working here among all the books, the centuries of information that had been passed down through the power of words and the printing press.

Working in Allison's bookshop was fine, but it didn't hold the connections to the past like a library did.

Mrs. Peacock, the remaining librarian, held forth from her glass-enclosed office, where she could keep a careful eye on her precious books and the patrons who visited her library. She was an older woman with a pronounced osteoarthritic hunch, who now sat behind her desk bundled in a heavy coat.

"Hi, Mrs. Peacock." Vivian knocked on the open door and stepped inside. "It's beginning to feel a lot like winter outside."

The librarian glanced up from her work and smiled. "Hello, dear. It's beginning to feel a lot like winter here in the library, too. I've asked the mayor again and again to find someone to check the heater. By the time January comes around, every book in the stacks will be frozen solid and so will I."

Chuckling, Vivian sat in the chair next to Mrs. Peacock's desk. "The least the town could do is buy you a pair of long johns."

"Honey, I'm already wearing them and praying the mayor doesn't spot them on my expense report."

Vivian laughed out loud. Despite Mrs. Peacock's physical limitations, she was as sharp as any winning contestant on *Jeopardy!* and had an amazing sense of humor.

"I came by to tell you about the read-a-thon we've started to help raise money for the animal shelter." Vivian handed her one form and placed the rest on her desk. "We're hoping you can encourage your patrons, particularly the youngsters, to sign up and get pledges."

Mrs. Peacock scanned the form quickly. "This is a terrific idea." She looked up. "I knew when

Mayor Langston mentioned the idea that you'd be perfect to put it all together. I'm sorry I didn't think of this myself—only to raise money for a new heating system, not for the shelter, however good a cause it is."

"Well, if this one is a success, maybe we can work on a read-a-thon for the library next."

"I may just hold you to that, my dear. Meanwhile, I'll see if I can stir up some support for the shelter."

As Chase closed up his shop that afternoon, the thought of eating his dinner upstairs held little appeal. Maybe he should drive into Wichita, have a night on the town. Or go to the Red Rooster. That was a lot closer, and the sky was beginning to look ominous with a coming storm.

He pulled down the shade on the doorway and switched off the overhead lights, leaving only the security lights on downstairs.

"G'night. G'night," Pepper squawked. "Sleep tight."

"Right, buddy. Too bad that guy who called about you hasn't called back." He lifted the cage to take Pepper with him.

"Errrrr," the bird purred, balancing on his swaying perch.

Feeling a surge of affection for the talkative, opinionated bird, Chase headed to his apartment.

Boyo raced up the stairs in front of him. He knew Fluff would come along when the mood struck her.

He recalled his meeting with Viv this morning and got a kick out of how excited she'd been over the read-a-thon. Who had ever heard of such a thing? Certainly nobody who worked at the warehouse had ever talked about one.

Life was a lot different, Chase thought as he stepped into his apartment, and a lot better in Bygones than he had experienced before he had moved here. If Fluff & Stuff didn't make it financially, he'd have to start over again. Probably working in another warehouse.

He'd have to move away from Bygones and Viv.

The thought of leaving made Chase sick to his stomach. Yet he knew, even if he stayed right here, he'd have to watch himself. She wanted a baby in the worst way. She was even willing to adopt one so she could have a family.

Chase couldn't go there. Not if it meant he'd be some child's father. He wouldn't do that to any kid. Not after what both he and his mother had suffered at the hands of his father.

The following morning, Chase drove to Danson Springs, where the nearest bank was located. He filled out the application for a new checking account, got the necessary signature forms and returned to Bygones by the time the bookstore was due to open.

The moment he stepped inside, he spotted Vivian.

Dressed in a long skirt and a deep red T-shirt, Viv was standing on a step stool, dusting the books on the top shelves of the bookcases. Her slender figure was perfectly proportioned. Very appealing. And strictly off-limits.

"Hey, good lookin'. Is your boss around?" He'd startled her, and she grabbed for something to steady herself. He reached up to help her keep her balance. "Careful now. No need to fall into my arms. People are bound to talk." Admittedly, he'd enjoy the experience, but it wasn't something he should wish for.

"They certainly are going to talk," Allison said from the doorway of the back room. "I wouldn't want you manhandling my employee."

"He's not manhandling me." Viv climbed down from the step stool, her face a bright pink. "He surprised me is all."

"Of course." Laughter sparkled in Allison's eyes. "In which case I'll just go about my business and not disturb you two."

"Actually, I came to see you, Allison."

Her head snapped toward him. "Oh?"

"You've been to the bank already this morning?" Viv asked.

"Yep. You know what they say, the early bird gets the worm. Though, if truth be told, I'm not very fond of worms for breakfast. I think they eat those in Thailand or somewhere."

"Vietnam. I understand they're crunchy." Allison wrinkled her nose. "What was it you wanted?"

Chase pulled out the bank's signature card from the pocket of his windbreaker. "I opened an account for the Happy Tales Read-a-thon. Viv made me treasurer, with your approval, I hope. I need a second name on the signature card. With two signatures required for a withdrawal, there'll be no chance of misappropriating whatever money we raise."

"Terrific idea." Allison quickly signed the card and handed it back to him.

"I'll do a weekly report of the income, and Viv can post the latest tally on the thermometer she's getting for the window."

"Allison ordered two, one for here and one for the shelter."

"I like that. I'll let Annabelle know." Chase liked working with Viv...and Allison...on this project. The shelter was close to his heart. Viv was, too. It was getting harder to not get closer to Viv with each passing day.

"Well, I best go open my shop. I wouldn't want the waiting crowd to be disappointed." He waved the card in the air and went out the door.

Running a pet store, helping out the animal shelter and working with Viv was a lot more fun than he'd ever had operating a forklift at the warehouse.

Late that afternoon, Vivian got a text message from Matt Garman with a link to the YouTube video he had created for the shelter fund-raiser.

"Already?" Wow, that was fast work for the young man.

She sat down at the bookshop's computer, went online and brought up the video. Upbeat music rose as a dancing beagle appeared on the screen followed by a skinny pirouetting Chihuahua and a wildly waving cocker spaniel. Matt provided the voice-over.

"Hey, dudes! Let's keep Hunter…and Pumpkin… and Buddy dancin'."

The scene flashed to the exterior of the shelter.

"Happy Havens Animal Shelter in the town of Bygones, Kansas, is their home. Times have been tough lately, so they need your help."

A picture of a mother cat nursing her kittens appeared, the kittens' heads bobbing in the same rhythm.

"Oscar is going to tell you what you gotta do."

A bulldog with a broad chest, top hat and twirling cane looked directly into the camera. "Hit it, boys," a deep voice said.

The howls, barks and whines of the caged shelter dogs rose in an earsplitting chorus. Information about the Happy Tales Read-a-thon scrolled slowly across the screen as quick shots of the dogs appeared in the background. Finally the phone number and address for the Happy Endings Bookstore appeared.

"Do it, man. Sign up. Keep 'em dancin'," the bulldog's voice-over ordered.

The screen faded to black.

"Oh, wow!" Vivian cried. "This is spectacular."

"What's spectacular?" Allison asked. She had been chatting with Whitney from the *Gazette* about the upcoming flyer to help bring business to Bygones for the holidays.

"Come see." Vivian pointed to the computer screen. "Matt made a video for the read-a-thon."

Allison and Whitney came over to stand behind the counter with Vivian.

Mrs. Aldridge, who had been helping her five-year-old son pick out a book for a friend's birthday, eased over to see what was going on, as well.

Vivian stepped out of Allison's way. "Just click on the arrow."

Whitney leaned in to see the screen.

"I've got to email Matt and tell him what a hit it is. And I'm going to call Chase, get him over here to see this."

She had just punched Chase's number into her cell when Mrs. Connolly walked into the bookshop.

With the phone at her ear, Vivian gestured for the school principal to take a look at the computer.

Chase answered the phone. "Hey, Viv. What's up?"

She swallowed a laugh and lowered her voice to a sultry tease. "Why don't you come over to the bookstore? I've got something to show you."

"That sounds like an invitation I wouldn't want to miss. Be right there." He ended the call.

With a secret smile playing around her lips, she joined the others at the computer. Chase was such a good guy. He had a way of making her feel all soft and feminine with his teasing comments. His voice could melt her insides, and his eyes could send a tremor through her body. She loved the feeling but feared she shouldn't get used to it. She sensed Chase, despite the way he used his sense of humor, had pulled back from their relationship.

Whitney asked, "What else have you got on this read-a-thon the video talked about?"

Allison handed her one of the forms. "We're trying to raise ten thousand dollars."

"Wow, that's pretty ambitious for Bygones," Whitney said.

Before Vivian had a chance to run the video again, Chase came hurrying in the door. He skidded to a halt. His mouth open, his expression dissipated into one of confusion. His eyes widened. "Looks like you invited a bunch of folks."

A tingle of pleasure rippled across Vivian's skin and laughter threatened. "Come see the video Matt put together for the read-a-thon. He's done a wonderfully clever bit of editing."

"Oh. That was fast."

Allison and Mrs. Connolly made room as he eased behind the counter to stand next to Vivian. He carried with him the fresh scent of the outdoors and the approaching rain.

"Watch this," she said.

She studied his expression as the video played. A smile curved his lips. Creases formed at the corners of his eyes as his smile broadened. He nodded his approval when the dogs howled and the video ended.

"Hey, that kid is all right, isn't he?"

"Who made the video?" Mrs. Connolly asked.

"Matt Garman," Chase answered.

Whitney scribbled the boy's name on her notepad.

"He's a very bright young man," Mrs. Connolly said. "But I had no idea he had this kind of talent."

"Josh said he'd help Matt." Vivian felt her phone vibrate in her pocket.

Mrs. Connolly's eyes widened. "Really? Well, wasn't that nice of him. Josh is such a quiet, interesting man." Her forehead furrowed in thought.

Vivian checked the caller ID on her phone. Her heart skipped a beat. "Excuse me. I have to take this call." She eased away from the others and went into the back room. There could be only two reasons why the Kansas Children's Services League would be calling her. She hoped it was the reason she had prayed for.

"Hel-lo." Her voice cracked.

"Ms. Duncan? This is Jacqueline Jackson— Jackie—from Children's Services. How are you today?"

"Fine." Ready to stop with the small talk and get to the reason the woman had called.

"Good. We have a situation here that may interest you." Jackie's refined tone hummed through the phone, racing toward Vivian at the speed of light. "We have a little boy named Theo. He's four months old. A cute, bright baby. His mother relinquished him at birth, however we were not able to place him immediately."

Holding the phone so tight her hand ached, Vivian sank onto the chair in the back room.

"He was born with a heart defect. We first had to make sure he was stabilized before his doctor could repair his heart."

Tears burned in Vivian's eyes. *Poor baby. So young to have surgery.* Love swelled in her chest for this unseen, unknown child. A baby she already longed to hold in her arms. To soothe his pain. To bring him comfort and love.

"Theo has been fostered by a woman trained in

medical procedures who also happens to live near the hospital," Jackie continued. "Now he is ready for a more permanent placement."

"Yes." Her throat was so tight that the word was little more than a whisper.

"I have to warn you that it is possible, now Theo is healthy, a relative may step forward to adopt him, in which case the relative would have preference over an unrelated adoptive parent."

Noooo.

"But if you think you are interested and willing, we would like to make a temporary placement with you until we can determine if other family members are willing and able to take on Theo's care."

"I... He wouldn't be mine permanently?"

"Not immediately. We may be able to change your status to a permanent placement at a later time. Please let me be clear. Many prospective adoptive parents don't want to accept a temporary placement. They know, rightly so, that they will become attached to the child. Giving a child up once he or she has lived with a new parent is extremely difficult emotionally. I will completely understand if you choose not to—"

"No. I mean yes. I want Theo." For a day or a month or the rest of his life. Tears edged down her cheeks. "I want to care for Theo for however long it's possible."

"I had the feeling you'd say that." Jackie's voice

held a smile. "Now, then, we'd like you to come to the league offices tomorrow morning..."

Jackie talked on about the details, but Vivian barely heard her. Tomorrow would be the first day of her life as a mother. Theo's *foster* mother, she corrected herself.

Dear heavenly Father, thank You. Thank You!

When the call ended, she sat for a moment before rejoining the others in the bookshop. When she stepped out of the back room, Allison hurried toward her.

"Vivian! What is it? Was that your mother on the phone? Is someone hurt?"

She shook her head. "I'm going to get a baby. At first I'll foster him and then maybe..." She sobbed and the tears rolled down her cheeks in a torrent. She drew a breath and hiccupped. "That was the adoption agency on the phone. The baby's name is Theo."

Allison, Mrs. Connolly and Mrs. Aldridge gathered around her, hugging her and talking all at once.

Even Whitney gave her a squeeze. "I'm so happy for you."

"I've already talked to Sam about this," Allison said, bubbling with excitement. "He says it's fine if I bring one of the twin's cribs down here and put it in the back room for your baby."

"How wonderful for you, my dear." Tears shone in Mrs. Connolly's eyes. "I do so love babies."

"I've still got some of Jeff's infant clothes and baby toys." Mrs. Aldridge drew her son closer to her. "I'll go through them and bring some down tomorrow."

Vivian blessed them all for sharing her excitement, but she could hardly speak. "That's wonderful. Thank you so much. All of you. I have to call my mother."

She took her phone to the back room again to place her call.

Her mother picked up on the second ring. "Hi, Viv. Are you still at work?"

"Yes." She started to cry again. "Mother, I'm getting a baby!"

"You're getting a—"

"A baby boy. His name is Theo. The adoption agency called. I'll be fostering him for now."

"Sophie! Go tell your dad Vivian's getting a baby!"

In the background, Vivian heard her younger sister squeal, then the back door of the house slammed shut, as Sophie went to find their father working somewhere around the farm.

Between her mother's tears and her own, Vivian managed to relate the phone call and what she knew about Theo.

"Mom, can you go with me to Wichita tomorrow?

"I wouldn't miss it for the world, honey." Her mother sniffed. "I adore babies, and this one is going to be so special."

By the time Vivian had talked to her sister and father, and returned to the front of the bookshop, everyone except Allison was gone.

Suddenly she realized Chase hadn't congratulated her. Or hugged her as she might have hoped.

He'd left without saying a word to her.

The joy that she was about to be a mother, if only temporarily, faded with the realization that one dream coming true could well mean the end of another dream she'd secretly held: that she and Chase could share a forever kind of love.

Back at the pet store, regret flowed through Chase like a frigid winter storm. Icicles of sorrow burrowed into his chest. The keening sound of mourning rose to his lips.

He couldn't be part of Viv's life if she was a mother. He couldn't be any child's father.

Growing up, everyone had said he looked just like his dad. The genes that had given him dark brown hair and long legs could also be the genes that turned him into a child beater.

Could turn him into the man his father had been.

Grief turned to anger and strummed inside him. Anger at his father. Anger at fate. Anger at himself because he was afraid he'd never be able to overcome the violent traits that his father could well have handed down to him.

The sins of the father shall be visited upon the son.

Chase didn't know if that was true. But for the sake of a child, he wasn't going to risk finding out.

Chapter Nine

Vivian arrived home to find her father's pickup parked in front of her house, the lights on inside and her dad carrying a dark walnut crib up the porch steps. He'd made the crib when Lisa, his eldest child, was born. Every child since, including Vivian, had slept in that crib…and had left teeth marks to prove it.

Her mother stepped out onto the porch, and Vivian hurried through the steadily falling rain to greet her.

"I'm so glad you're home," Mindy Duncan said. "Marcia Toliver is bringing over her grandson's car seat. He doesn't need it anymore. Beth Ann has a high chair, though I don't suppose Theo will need that right away. Deborah is bringing clothes and a playpen. Everyone is so excited for you."

She opened her arms and Vivian stepped into them for a hug. "Sounds to me like you've been on the phone quite a bit since we talked."

"Oh, you know how it is. Good news spreads fast." Her mother's infectious laugh spurred Vivian's similar response. Their joyous duet rose to the heavens, filled with praise and gratitude.

"Mom," Vivian said, stepping out of her mother's embrace. "We have to be careful not to get carried away. At this point I'm only a foster parent. I may not get to keep Theo."

"I know, dear. I'm just going to relish the moment and leave the rest up to God."

Vivian knew she had to do that, too. Have faith that she was on the path the Lord wanted her to travel. But it was hard when *she* wanted to be a mother so much she could feel her heart reaching out to tiny Theo with all the love she could muster.

They walked inside together. Vivian's sister Sophie, a reddish-blond eighteen-year-old, sat cross-legged on the floor playing with a toy that mooed or barked or gobbled when she pressed on a particular button.

"I used to love playing with this." She pushed on the button next to the cow.

"You can't remember back that far," Vivian said.

"Sure I can." Sophie pressed another button, this time for a pig. *Oink oink.*

"You were only two years old when you played with that."

Sophie tossed her long hair over her shoulder.

"It's just like having perfect pitch. I have a perfect memory."

Laughing, feeling overwhelmed and a little frightened by the reality of it all, she gave her sister an affectionate flick of a finger on her head. "My perfect sister."

Ducking her head out of the way of any further attacks, Sophie cried, "Ouch. Stop that."

Dad came out of the second bedroom. "You want the crib set up in here?"

"I guess so. But won't Roger keep the baby awake?" Vivian asked. Why hadn't she thought about that when she had bought Roger? She'd been thinking about adopting then. She shouldn't have—

"Gene, why don't you move the desk and Roger's cage out here?" Vivian's mother suggested. "There's room in the dining area. Then we can get her a low dresser to keep the baby things in and use for a changing table. I think there's one in the attic that will do."

Starting to shiver, Vivian hugged herself. "Mom, this is like a dream. I'm so excited, and at the same time, I'm so scared. What if I'm terrible at taking care of a baby?"

Mindy Duncan wrapped her arms around her daughter. "Viv, honey, you've been mothering one child or another ever since the twins were born, and you were still a toddler yourself. You're going to be a wonderful mother."

"If I am, it will be because of everything you taught me."

A sheen of tears filmed her mother's eyes. "The best thing is I get to cuddle another baby."

"And spoil Theo just like you do Lisa's little girl."

They both laughed then went to help Gene move Roger and his cage. They barely had the crib set up when Marcia Toliver, a longtime friend of the family, appeared with a car seat, which Vivian would use tomorrow to bring Theo home.

Home. Having a baby gave new meaning to that simple word.

Sophie had given up playing with the baby toys and had picked up a book from the end table. "What's with *Quantrill's Kansas?* Are you into the Civil War now?"

"A small publisher in Topeka sent me that book to review for my new blog," Vivian explained.

Sophie's eyes widened. "You're doing a blog?"

"About heartland authors and their books. I hope to generate enough interest that I can eventually get a following and some advertising. There's a reenactors group that performs shows about Quantrill and his mounted troop."

"Wow, Viv. That sounds, like, so twenty-first-century cool."

A laugh caught in Vivian's throat. "I sure hope so."

Soon Beth Ann and Deborah drove up, bringing a high chair, a playpen and two big boxes of baby clothes.

Sophie was like a kid on Christmas morning, checking out the tiny T-shirts and sweaters, denim overalls and sleepers.

"Oh, these are so sweet," she cooed. "I want to have a baby, too."

"You're too young!" Vivian and her mother chorused.

The eighteen-year-old glared at them. "At least I should be able to go with you to pick up Theo."

"Tomorrow is a school day," Mindy pointed out.

"Missing one day wouldn't hurt. It's no big deal. I am sort of going to be Theo's aunt, aren't I?"

"You can come visit tomorrow after school," Vivian promised her sister. "We should be back home by then."

That seemed to mollify Sophie. For the moment.

By the time they'd established a certain amount of organization and her family and friends had gone home, Vivian's adrenaline had slowed to normal. She was exhausted. Even so she didn't sleep well and was glad when it was morning and time to pick up her mother for the trip to Wichita.

As Vivian started her car, she thought of Chase. He'd be up by now, feeding the puppies and kittens at Fluff & Stuff, and getting ready to open the store.

While she loved her mother and wanted her to be

there for moral support, this trip to Wichita would be very different if she and Chase were going to pick up their baby together.

She drew a stuttering breath and blinked away the burn of tears in her eyes. *Don't ask for things you know you can't have.*

This was her day. And Theo's. She was going to cherish every moment so she'd be able to tell Theo about it when he grew up. *If* she was allowed to become his adoptive mom, she sternly reminded herself. Not that she was listening very closely to that negative voice that kept her dreams in check.

As soon as she pulled up in front of her parents' house, her mother came running out and got into the car. She carried her purse and a large paper sack, which she put into the backseat next to the car seat.

"Gene reminded me to bring the camera." An excited glow on her cheeks, her mother snapped her seat belt in place. "Agnes Springer came by last night with diapers and a couple of bottles. She didn't know what kind of formula the baby might need, so we'll have to stop for that somewhere in the city."

Vivian turned the car around and headed out the long drive from the house to the road. "That was very sweet of Agnes, but Jackie at the agency said she'd give me enough supplies to last for a few days."

"Oh, well, better to have too much than too little."

It took about an hour and a half to get to Wichita on a good day. Longer with Friday morning traffic as they got closer to the city.

With each passing mile, Vivian's anxiety and excitement increased. Would Theo like her? What if he cried when she held him? Would Jackie decide she wasn't suited to be a foster mother?

On the outskirts of the sun-dappled city, residential tracts replaced open fields and farmland. The Wichita skyline rose in front of them with high-rise buildings and church steeples. Vivian turned off the highway into an older part of town where the agency was located in a renovated three-story house constructed of stone.

"We're here." She pulled into the parking lot. Her mouth was dry, her palms wet and her stomach knotted.

When she didn't exit the car right away, her mother said, "You know, if you've changed your mind, I'll be happy to foster little Theo myself. I miss having babies around."

Vivian snorted. "No, I haven't changed my mind." But she was suffering from a bad case of nerves.

Once inside the office, a grandmotherly receptionist greeted them with a welcoming smile. Minutes later Jackie, a slender woman in her fifties, led them back to her private office. Photos of happy parents holding babies adorned the walls, which were painted a lively turquoise with white trim.

Vivian had a moment of panic as she glanced around the welcoming office. Where was Theo? Had a relative already claimed him?

She listened for the sound of a crying baby and didn't hear so much as a peep. Only the rhythmic sound of computer keys clicking away somewhere nearby reached her ears.

Jackie sat down behind her desk. Vivian and her mother sat opposite her in two comfortable guest chairs. Unable to relax, Vivian sat on the edge of her seat. Her heart thundered and her breathing was unusually shallow.

"I know you're anxious to meet Theo," Jackie said, her smile understanding. "But there are a few details we need to go over."

Through a veil of fog, Vivian heard Jackie talk about the responsibilities of a foster parent, care for Theo's incision and his need for regular checkups. She gave Vivian papers describing Theo's medical history, his usual schedule and finally documents she had to sign.

She didn't read a word they said. She simply signed the forms. In her fuzzy-minded state, she wouldn't be able to make sense of the legal jargon anyway.

All she wanted to do was hold Theo in her arms.

"All right." Jackie pushed back her chair. "Let's

go meet Theo. He is one of my favorites. You're going to love him."

But would Theo love her?

Once she had him in her arms, would he be taken away from her?

Jackie took them to a room that looked very much like an oversize nursery with three cribs, each of them with a mobile rotating slowly above it.

The sight of little arms and legs encased in a light blue onesie outfit waving in the air drew her to the crib on the right. Her heart racing, she peered down at the child.

"Oh, he's beautiful." Big brown eyes above chubby cheeks gazed up at her. He smiled and cooed and continued to wave his hands. His thick brown hair looked as though an inexperienced barber had taken pinking shears to his head. The result was a mishmash of hair of various lengths that went every which way.

A powerful wave of love flooded her body. A force so strong it filled her every cell, leaving her with no way to speak or even breathe. The sensation touched her very soul, and she knew this love for Theo was a gift from God.

She reached out her hands to Theo, and he reached for hers. "Hello, Theo. Did you know you get to come live with me?" She prayed hers would be a forever home for him, but if not, she prayed for the strength to give him all the love he needed for as long as she got to keep him.

Picking him up, she held him tight. Feeling his weight in her arms. Smelling the sweet scent of baby powder. Brushing her face against his soft, cubby cheek. His neck was strong, and he held his head high.

A camera flashed. In slow motion, the baby blinked his eyes.

"I love you, Theo. I love you more than the moon and stars. More than the oceans and the earth." Vivian repeated the words she had heard a thousand times as her own mother had held her in her arms. "And God loves you, too."

He bounced and stretched his legs. His tiny hand grabbed on to a hank of her hair.

Again Vivian's mother snapped a picture.

"Ouch," Vivian whispered, trying to dislodge his grip as she laughed at him. "Go easy on my hair." She buzzed his neck with a kiss.

He giggled, a rollicking laugh that surprised him and made Vivian cry with joy.

"Looks like you two have already bonded." Jackie stood a few feet away, giving Vivian the time to assimilate this joyous moment.

Turning, Vivian nodded, her vision blurred with unshed tears. "He's wonderful. Perfect."

"Why don't you let your mother hold Theo for a

minute while we go over the supplies I'll be sending home with you," Jackie suggested.

Vivian's mother held out her arms for Theo.

It was all Vivian could do to relinquish her glorious baby for even a second.

"I won't steal him or drop him, I promise," her mother said with a loving smile.

Vivian relented, handing her baby into the outstretched arms of her mother.

Sometime later, after Jackie had checked to make sure they had installed the car seat correctly, Vivian drove away from the adoption agency. Her heart was so full, she kept expecting it to burst.

If Chase could experience a moment like this, she knew he'd fall in love with Theo, too. How could such a good, kind man do otherwise.

If only he'd give himself a chance.

Between customers on Saturday, Chase kept glancing out Fluff & Stuff's front window hoping to see Viv's car go by. He supposed she was at home. She'd want at least one day off to get used to the baby.

He imagined she'd be good at mothering. A natural. Her kindness and gentle ways, the lyrical sound of her laughter, would captivate any baby.

Just as she captivated him.

Frowning, he set that thought firmly aside.

Growing closer to Viv was not on his to-do list. Staying clear of her was closer to the truth.

"Pepper want a cracker. Pepper want a cracker." The parrot hopped down to the floor of his cage and rummaged through the newspaper he had shredded.

"Pepper's going to be a fat bird if you keep eating so much," Chase admonished the bird.

"Poor Pepper," the parrot crooned.

Chase hated to admit it, but the foolish bird was beginning to grow on him. Becoming a part of his "family." He held up a cracker, and Pepper snatched it from his hand with his agile claw.

"Good birdie. Good birdie." Balancing on one leg, Pepper took a delicate bite out of the cracker.

"Right." Chase looked out the window again. He wondered how Viv was getting along. If the baby had slept through the night. Or kept Viv awake.

Either way it didn't matter, he thought, as he greeted a customer who wanted to buy some dog chow. Chase wouldn't have anything to do with Viv's baby.

It was better that way. Safer for all of them.

After being inundated with visitors who came by her house on Friday afternoon and Saturday, Vivian hoped for a quieter Sunday. She bundled Theo in a warm blanket and secured him in his car seat for the short ride to church. Afterward they would have supper with her family. But first she would present Theo to the Lord in His house and give thanks for her many blessings.

Allison greeted Vivian even before she got to the church door.

"Oh, let me see that precious baby. I'm so sorry I couldn't get away yesterday to meet him."

Juggling a diaper bag on one arm, Vivian managed to lift a corner of the blanket that covered Theo's face. His big brown eyes met hers, and a bubble escaped his rosebud mouth. "Hi, sweetheart. Somebody wants to say hello."

"Look at those cheeks!" Allison touched one with her fingertip. "Isn't he the cutest little baby you've ever seen?"

Maternal pride swelled in Vivian's chest. "I think so." God's perfect little creature.

"You are so blessed." Allison enveloped both Vivian and Theo in a group hug. "You're going to bring him to the bookstore with you tomorrow, aren't you?"

"If you're sure it won't be too disruptive. My mother said she'd babysit if I needed her." In fact, her mother had been visibly disappointed that she wouldn't be babysitting Theo every day of the week.

"You'll need your mother more when this little one starts crawling around and being more active. For now, he'll be just fine at the bookshop."

Sam appeared, apparently having safely delivered the twins to the preschool class. He hooked his arm around Allison's waist and peered down at the baby. "Cute kid. Looks like he's going to be a football player. Probably go pro right from high school."

Vivian laughed. "I think it's a little early to decide Theo's future career."

She continued into the church, where Mrs. Connolly stopped her to get a peek at the baby. That drew a crowd of women, who hovered around Vivian, plying her with praise for Theo and more advice than any new mother could handle.

"Adorable! By the time he's twelve, you'll be chasing the girls away."

"Is he sleeping through the night? I always fed my babies cereal before bed so they wouldn't wake up too soon."

"Such a big boy. Can he roll over yet?"

They were all blocking the aisle, so Vivian edged away, smiling, and found a place in the back pew in case Theo started to fuss. She removed Theo's blanket so he wouldn't get overheated and settled him in her lap.

"We have to be quiet, sweetie. This is God's house. He's looking down on us right now." She touched her finger to Theo's lips to hush him.

He waved his arms and legs, gurgling. Then he let loose with his newly discovered laugh just as the worship team paused before beginning the opening hymn.

Everyone within three rows turned in Vivian's direction. Heat rose to her cheeks even as they all smiled knowingly at her.

The gray-haired gentleman in the pew in front of her leaned back, his smile touching his aging eyes and softening his weatherworn wrinkles earned from a lifetime of working his fields. "It's always nice to hear from a new member of the congregation."

With a grateful smile, she thanked him for his understanding.

Lifting Theo to her shoulder, Vivian stood with the congregation as they sang "O Life That Makest All Things New." She rejoiced for Theo and her new life as a foster mother.

As she sang, she glanced around the sanctuary. Her gaze fell on a man standing about midway to the altar. Her breath caught. He looked so familiar. The same brown hair. The same set of his shoulders. Could that be Chase?

She stared hard, willing the man to turn so she could get a look at his face. She didn't think Chase was a regular churchgoer. He'd never mentioned attending a church. But if he were here now…

The man turned to the woman standing beside him, providing Vivian with a quick glimpse of his profile. Not Chase. Only a creation of her imagination. A stranger.

A frisson of disappointment chilled her and she hugged Theo more tightly.

Three days since she'd seen Chase. Already she felt the loss. His absence from her life.

As the hymn ended, she sat down and straightened her spine. The Lord had given her Theo. She had no right to ask for more.

Please, Lord, don't take Theo away from me.

Vivian arrived at the bookstore late for work Monday morning, loaded down with diapers, changes of outfits for Theo, baby rattles to amuse him if he got bored, extra pacifiers if he got fussy and bottles of formula when he got hungry. With all of that, she'd probably forgotten something she'd need later.

"How's the new mama doing?" Allison asked.

"Well, I'm not officially his mother." She quirked her lips into a half smile, mentally adding *yet.* "And by the way, do you have any idea how much stuff it takes to keep a baby happy for a whole day?"

Allison eyed the overflowing diaper bag hanging from Vivian's shoulder. "Looks like a lot."

"Tell me about it." Vivian hiked the diaper bag onto the counter. "Sorry I'm late. It took me forever to pack all of this stuff plus feed Theo and get him dressed."

"Here. Give him to me while you get yourself organized." Allison held out her arms, and Theo went willingly into them. A big dollop of slobber landed on Allison's long-sleeve T-shirt, leaving a damp spot.

Vivian quickly wiped it away with a dry washcloth. "Sorry about that. I think he's teething."

"Don't worry about it. The twins have already done worse to me and my clothes. Comes with the territory." She jiggled Theo up and down, and cooed at him. Theo responded with "B-aaa. B-aaa."

"Listen, he's already trying to talk," Vivian said.

"Of course he is. B-aaa, b-aaa," Allison echoed as she walked to the front of the store with Theo in her arms. "I'm your auntie Alli. Did you know that?"

Smiling, Vivian dug a blanket and a bottle out of the diaper bag. Theo would be ready for his morning nap pretty soon. She wanted to be prepared when the time came.

A moment later, she heard the shop door open and Allison talking with Bea, the mail carrier. By the time Vivian went out front, Bea was gone and Allison was standing behind the counter.

"Look at this, will you?" Allison held up a packet of envelopes. "There must be at least a dozen letters here addressed to Happy Tales Read-a-thon."

"Really? No one could have already read their

books or gotten pledges. I just distributed the entry forms late last week."

"I know." Frowning, Allison ripped open the first envelope. A check fell out. "Twenty-five dollars."

"I didn't expect we'd get results so soon." She took Theo back from Allison so she had the use of two hands to open the envelopes.

The checks kept coming with each letter. Twenty-five dollars. One check for a hundred dollars. A five-dollar bill.

Allison read the return addresses. "Springfield, Missouri. Wichita. Fort Worth, Texas. How did these people hear about the read-a-thon?"

Puzzled, they looked at each other.

"Matt's YouTube video!" Vivian blurted out.

She slipped behind the counter and went online on the computer, typing in the address of the video. She scrolled down the screen and gasped.

"Allison! Matt's video has more than a thousand hits." By Bygones standards, that was virtually going viral. It could mean hundreds of people sending donations for the shelter. How incredible! How very wonderful. Far better than she had ever anticipated.

"I've got to call Chase. He needs to see this."

Chapter Ten

Chase raced out of Fluff & Stuff at a dead run, leaving a customer standing at the cash register. Viv had sounded so excited on the phone he couldn't understand what she was trying to tell him. Something about hits?

Had someone hit her? Or Theo? Whatever it was, Chase would put a stop to it.

He burst into the bookshop and came to an abrupt halt.

Standing behind the counter, Viv looked fine. In fact, she looked beautiful. Her blue eyes bright, her cheeks pink… And she glowed with happiness holding a baby firmly propped on her hip.

"I guess that's Theo, huh?" he asked inanely. What other baby would she be holding?

"Yes, but that's not why I called you. Come back here and let me show you the computer."

He eased behind the counter. The baby—Theo—

was trying hard to get his whole fist in his mouth. Drool crept out around the edges. He pumped his feet, which somehow dislodged his hand from its goal. His eyes widened, and he stared right at Chase as though he'd been at fault.

"Hi," Chase said, feeling foolish.

Theo gave him a big juicy raspberry, startling himself. Then he laughed the most infectious sound Chase had ever heard.

Chase felt his lips curving into a smile. "Think you're pretty smart, don't you, kiddo?"

Theo laughed again, pumped his legs and leaned toward Chase. He froze. Was he supposed to take the baby? And do what with him? He'd never held a baby in his life. He hardly knew which end was up. Probably something he should know before he did anything rash like try to hold a squirming, kicking kid.

"Chase, I want you to look at Matt's video," Viv said, having missed the exchange between Chase and the baby. "See how many hits it's gotten already."

Slowly he dragged his gaze away from Theo. "Hits?"

"Yes, the number of people who have watched the video. It's gone viral."

He stepped closer to Viv to peer at the screen where Viv was pointing. "A thousand?" Theo grabbed Chase's shirt in his gooey hand and tugged.

Chase looked down at the tiny little fist twisted in the fabric of his shirt. The kid had a good hard grip. Strong. Amazing he could hold on so tight when he was so little.

"Isn't that incredible? And look at this." Viv held up a handful of envelopes. "We're already getting contributions for the shelter."

Allison, who was standing on the other side of Viv, said, "There's almost five-hundred-dollars' worth of checks and cash in those envelopes."

"Wow. That's as much as I'd hoped we'd raise in total. I never expected—" His cell phone rang. Frowning, he gently pried Theo's grip from his shirt, pulled the phone from his pocket and checked the caller's number. "Hey, Annabelle. What's up?"

"The UPS guy just delivered a fifty-pound bag of dog food for the shelter." She spoke in a staccato voice that rose in pitch. In the background, dogs barked with the same excitement. "Can you believe it?"

"Yeah, I can. The video's gone viral. Folks are already sending in contributions." Stunned, he looked at the envelopes and then at Viv. All grins, she nodded.

"The Lord be praised!" Annabelle said.

Chase had never been religious, but he figured God must have had a hand in this. How else could the video have reached so many people so quickly? Matt, apparently with Josh's help, was a genius.

"Annabelle, let me get back to you. I've got to check on the contributions that came in this morning." He ended the call. Both Allison and Viv were looking at him.

"The shelter just had a fifty-pound bag of dog food delivered."

"This is so awesome." Theo started fussing and Viv bounced the baby on her hip as naturally as if she'd been a mother forever. She kissed the kid on his plump little cheek.

Chase tried not to feel jealous.

"I've got to feed Theo and put him down for his nap," she said.

Allison said, "You go ahead. Chase and I will count up the money. Then he can make out the bank deposit slip."

"Right." He needed to get back to the pet store, too. By now his customer could've walked out in a huff. Or she could've left the money for the fancy dog collar on the counter. Folks around Bygones seemed particularly honest. Maybe that was another reason he liked living here. "Let me go to my store and get a ledger. I'll be right back."

"See you later." Viv's smile made her look like a woman fulfilled as she ducked into the back room.

Chase suppressed the urge to follow her. To

watch her feed the baby. Help her get him ready for his nap. But that made no sense at all.

Mentally, he groaned. She was the temptation he neither needed nor wanted and yet couldn't seem to avoid.

On Tuesday Chase picked up another half dozen checks at the bookshop. The big red thermometer in the bookshop window had edged up from the bottom.

Wednesday, Viv handed him a handful of envelopes she hadn't had time to open yet.

"We had several parents come by to pick up read-a-thon forms and buy books for their children to read." She had Theo sitting in an infant seat on the counter, where he had a good view of the goings-on in the bookshop, including the activities of several customers. It looked as if the discount flyers for businesses in Bygones that had been distributed were drawing folks into town. Several customers had come in to shop at the pet store for pet gifts, bringing the flyer with them.

He was really glad Allison had come up with such a good marketing idea.

Chase eyed the baby sitting on the counter. Something about those big brown eyes tickled him. Like the kid was supervising the whole store. Impulsively, he buzzed his lips.

Theo jerked. His head turned so he could focus

hard on Chase. Theo blew a big bubble that popped all over his face as if to say, "See how smart I am."

"Yeah, I see you, kiddo." Chase started opening the envelopes Viv had given him, pulling out the checks and setting them aside.

A customer came to the counter with a couple of books to buy. They looked like romance novels. Chase stepped aside to give her room while Viv rang up the sale.

Theo fussed and squirmed in his seat.

Another customer wanted to buy a mystery she was giving to her father for Christmas.

Viv glanced at her baby and then at Chase. "He's getting fussy. Would you mind picking him up and holding him for a minute while I take care of Mrs. Carmichael?"

"Me?" Chase's eyes widened. He went very still.

"Yes, you. Theo might drool a little, but he won't bite you."

No, of course not. The kid didn't have any teeth yet. Did he?

Gingerly, Chase undid the strap that held Theo safely in the infant seat. The baby kicked at him. "Easy, kid. This is all new to me."

Using two hands, Chase picked up Theo under the arms and held him away from his body. Little chubby legs swam in the air.

"Hold him close to you, up against your chest," Viv prompted. "He'll feel more secure that way."

But would Chase feel secure?

He pulled Theo to him. Immediately, the baby dropped his head to Chase's shoulder and heaved a sigh.

Chase felt something stir inside him. A loosening of tight muscles. A sense of contentment. The realization that holding a baby was downright pleasant and not so hard.

He pressed his face against Theo's little head. The baby's hair was as soft as a downy chick and smelled of a sweet shampoo, his plump body warm enough to ward off a winter chill.

Slowly, not wanting to disturb Theo, he began patting his back and rubbing his hand up and down the baby's spine.

Viv finished taking care of her customers. Chase didn't want to give Theo back to her. Not yet. He wanted the sensation of holding this small living, breathing creature close to him.

"He needs to take his bottle before I put him down for his nap," Viv said. "Would you like to feed him?"

He swallowed hard. "Uh, no." He eased Theo off his shoulder and handed the baby to Viv. "I've got to get back to Fluff & Stuff."

"Of course," she said. She met his gaze, and he knew she could see right through him. See his fears. Somehow see his past. "Maybe next time."

Chase didn't think so. He had to make Viv understand why he was terrified of being a father. Of ever taking responsibility for a child. That was the fair thing for him to do. For both of them.

Chase snatched up the checks and envelopes and fled out the door. How in the world would he ever make Viv understand that he couldn't be the man she wanted him to be?

He rubbed his hand over the scar on his chin. A scar he saw in the mirror every morning when he shaved. And the memories that went with it.

He'd have to make her see the truth of who he was.

In the back room, Vivian gazed down at Theo as he gobbled down the formula in his bottle. Love and gratitude filled her soul.

"Greedy little guy, aren't you?"

His heavy eyelids lifted just enough that he could look up at her, then closed again as he continued to suck every precious drop from the bottle.

Chase had looked so uncomfortable, so on edge, when he had picked Theo up. For a moment Vivian had been afraid he'd drop the baby. Or have a seizure. Poor man. He'd certainly never been around babies much.

But when Chase had put Theo on his shoulder, Vivian had seen something change in him. Lines of tension around his lips eased. He got sort of a dreamy look in his eyes. But when she'd asked him if he wanted to feed the baby, panic had set in, and his pupils had turned almost black.

While she could understand, marginally, that he worried about her raising a baby on her own, she suspected a deeper concern. Perhaps a darker reason than the fact that his mother had struggled as a single parent.

A reason he hadn't yet shared with her.

When Chase got back to his store, he couldn't seem to do anything right. He spilled a whole bag of Super Ball doggie toys that bounced down every aisle, delighting Boyo with a good chase.

Somehow he had to come clean with Viv. Tell her the whole truth about his past. But how? And when?

He fretted about it overnight. Thursday morning he kept a sharp eye on the comings and goings along Main Street. Midweek was often slow. Surely there'd be a time when he could catch Viv alone.

Finally he saw Allison's car drive down the street. Viv would be on her own at the shop for at least a little while. No customers seemed to be around.

A lump formed in his throat as he turned the sign on his shop door to Be Back Soon, locked up and hurried to Happy Endings. His hands felt clammy as he stepped into the bookstore.

Standing behind the counter with Theo on her

hip, she looked up from a catalog she was reading. "Hey, Chase. Didn't expect to see you this morning."

He was struck again by how natural she looked with a baby in her arms. She could mother a half dozen kids, and it wouldn't faze her. That would terrify Chase.

"I was just looking through this catalogue for Christmas things for Theo," she said. "There are so many fun toys these days. It's going to be hard to choose."

He frowned, trying to remember what she'd said the morning the adoption agency had called her. "Didn't I hear you say you're temporarily fostering Theo? That a relative might want to adopt him?"

"That's what the social worker said, but I have to pray that won't happen." She rubbed her cheek against the baby's hair.

"Maybe you shouldn't get too attached to Theo. If they take him away from you—"

"Chase, love isn't something you turn on and off like a light switch. I love Theo. That wouldn't stop if I had to give him up."

"I know you well enough to know you'd be hurt if you lost Theo." Probably beyond hurt. More like devastated. She was one of those rare women who, once they gave their heart, didn't take it back.

"That doesn't change the fact that I love him." Setting the catalogue aside, she eased Theo into his infant seat on the counter. "I have feelings for you, too, Chase. If you suddenly left town and went back to Wichita, I'd still have those feelings. When you care about someone, you don't stop caring simply because they're gone."

The world beneath Chase's feet seemed to shift. Viv cared about him? Sure, he'd felt they were becoming good friends, but she was talking about more than that. More than he was capable of giving?

"Did you have something about the read-a-thon you wanted to talk about?" she asked, as she took a seat near Theo.

Chase stuffed his hands in his pockets. Yeah, what did he want to say? And how could he say it when she'd told him that she had feelings for him?

"I, um…" She was looking up at him expectantly, her blue eyes wide with interest. He cleared a lump from his throat. Searched for the right words. Tried to find stable ground in his shifting world. "I told you about being raised by a single mom. But I didn't tell you why she was raising me alone. You need to know the truth about me so you'll understand."

"Truth?" She cocked her head, listening.

Chase took a deep breath as the memories, the terrible images, came back to him. He had to make her understand without hurting her.

"My father abused my mother. Sometimes he

beat her so bad, he'd break her arm or a rib. But he never hit her in the face so nobody knew. Except me." Tears burned in his eyes. Hate scorched through his belly.

"I was too little to do anything about it," he continued. His remembered sense of helplessness still had the power to drive him to his knees. "Mom would make me go to my room. I'd hide under my bed and cover my ears." She had tried so hard not to cry out, but Chase had heard her. Heard her sobbing after his father had left to go to a bar and join his buddies.

"That's terrible," Viv said. "And that's why she left him and raised you alone?"

"She didn't leave for a long time." He paced over to a bookcase filed with mysteries, but he didn't read the titles. He stood where he could measure her reaction. "Mom was too afraid to leave. He had told her that he'd track her down. And kill her."

When Chase had heard that threat, he had believed it. So had his mother.

"I'm so sorry, Chase. It must have been awful for both you and your mother."

"Yeah, it was." He ran his palm over his face trying to erase the memories. Impossible. They were etched in his brain like someone had taken a chisel to the inside of his head. "When I was about nine, I tried to stop my dad from hitting Mom. I hung on to his arm and tried to kick him. He got pretty mad."

"He hit you?" Her eyes wide, her mouth open, she looked as though the thought of a father hitting a child was the most appalling thing she could think of.

Chase nodded. "That was the first time. After that he'd beat me with a stick. Throw me across the room." Involuntarily, he rubbed the scar on his chin remembering how he had hit the corner of an end table. Blood had gushed everywhere. His mother had screamed. So had Chase. "I couldn't do anything right after that. He'd lay into me for no reason at all."

"Couldn't your mother—"

"She tried. He'd just turn on her then. She ended up in the hospital a couple of times when she'd tried to stop him."

"I wish she'd reported him to the police."

"The police showed up two or three times. The neighbors reported them fighting." He shook his head. "Mom was too scared to say anything. She always denied there was a problem.

"Finally, when he'd beaten me real good, she'd had enough. When he fell into a drunken stupor as he usually did, she packed us a suitcase, took whatever money he had in his wallet and the car keys. She drove us to the bus station, and we got on the first bus out of town. We got as far as Wichita before we ran out of money. Then she started looking for a job."

"I am so glad she got you away from that man. He might have killed you both."

Chase's gaze slid to Theo, who had fallen asleep in the infant seat on the counter. The picture of innocence.

"I think he would have, given enough time. He was evil, Viv. Pure evil."

"Knowing you, knowing what a gentle, good person you are, I never would have guessed you'd had such an awful background. I'm glad you told me."

"I didn't tell you to get your sympathy or anything like that. I wanted you to know why I'll never bring a child into this world. I'll never be a father."

Her forehead creased. "I don't understand. Just because your father—"

"I carry my father's genes, Viv." He paced back to the counter to look at Theo. So sweet. He could never risk such an innocent life. Not when he knew how brutal a man could be.

"That doesn't mean you're like your father. In fact, I'd say you were the exact opposite."

"How do you know? My mother told me he hadn't beaten her when they first got married. She'd been in love with him. And then he changed. He became a monster." He looked away, focusing on the books on the shelves, the horn of plenty on top of the bookcase with plastic fruit and vegetables spilling out of it. "What if I'm a monster, too?"

"You aren't! You couldn't be. You're selling

yourself short, Chase. I believe with all my heart you'd be a wonderful father if you had the chance. I have faith in you."

The muscle in his jaw clenched. Faith wouldn't change who he was, where he came from. "Faith is your department, Viv, not mine."

"Please, Chase." She lowered her voice to a plea. "What if I have enough faith for both of us?"

He nearly reached out to her but held back. "I'm sorry, Viv. It's no good. I can't be the man you want me to be. I'm too damaged to be what you and Theo need."

He forced himself to turn away. To walk to the door and leave. His body felt as though he'd been through a battle. Or been beaten within an inch of his life.

At least now Viv knew the truth.

Vivian got up to stop Chase from leaving the bookstore, but it was too late.

"Oh, Chase…"

How could he possibly believe he was a monster like his father? Chase didn't have a cruel bone in his body. She was sure of it.

Despite his lack of experience with babies, he'd been gentle and loving with Theo when she'd asked him to pick up the baby the other day. He'd always been friendly with the kids who showed up at Fluff & Stuff on the way home from school. She'd never once seen him lose patience with anyone, much less a child.

He was even patient with Pepper, whose squawking could easily become downright annoying.

Chase had had so much pain in his eyes, as though he could still feel his father beating him. He'd touched his chin, rubbing the scar there, and Vivian realized his father had caused that scar.

What a terrible thing for a father to do!

Maybe Chase had told her about his past, not because of his unreasonable fear of being a father, but because he wanted to keep his distance from her. He wanted to bring to a halt whatever relationship they had developed.

He didn't see them together in the future.

That she had come to care for him, deeply, didn't matter. In fact, it probably frightened him.

Smoothing Theo's untamed hair, she fought the tears that threatened. Chase wasn't going to give her a chance. Give *them* a chance to see where their relationship could go. He was using Theo as an excuse.

She didn't miss the irony. Two men had dumped her because she couldn't have a baby. Now Chase had dumped her because she actually had a baby. At least temporarily.

She drew in a painful breath. That was so unfair.

Chapter Eleven

Carrying Pepper in his cage, Chase went downstairs the next morning to feed the puppies. As he hung the cage in place by the front counter, Pepper crooned, "Morn…ing. Morn…ing."

"Yeah, buddy, it's morning all right." But not necessarily a good one.

Faith. He'd never had much confidence in the vague concept of believing in something he couldn't see or touch, he thought, as he walked to the back of the shop to greet the current batch of puppies.

He'd tried to have faith his dad wouldn't hit him again. He'd tried to believe his mother wouldn't always have to work two jobs just to pay the rent.

Reality had always topped faith. It still did.

"Bad bird! Bad bird!" Pepper began to squawk at the top of his voice.

"I'll be there in a minute, Pepper. Keep your feathers on."

"Come again! Come again! Come again!" Pepper repeated the phrase over and over.

"Be quiet!" The puppies rolled and tumbled away from Chase. "Not you guys. I'm yelling at Pepper." He scooped up some dry puppy chow and refilled their dish.

"Fire! Fire! Help me! Help me!"

What was wrong with that ridiculous bird? He never carried on like that. Not since his owner's son had brought him to the pet shop to be sold.

Disgusted, and angry with himself about not being good enough for Viv, he stalked over to the bird and glared at him.

"Help me! Help me!"

He was about to give Pepper what for when he saw the problem. Not a problem with Pepper, but the smear of red paint across the shop's front window.

"What in the world?" Unlocking the door, he stepped out onto the sidewalk into the cold morning air. Someone had painted a big red *X* across the window. He clenched his fists in anger and frustration. Why hadn't the police caught the vandal yet?

He whirled as though the culprit might still be hanging around to admire his work. But the only person on the street was Allison, looking at her own shop window, which was crisscrossed with a matching *X*.

"Pretty annoying, isn't it?" Chase strolled down

the sidewalk toward Allison. A sharp wind tugged at her long skirt and whipped the tips of her long brown hair across her face.

"I'll say. I'm going to call Joe Sheridan right now. He really has to do something about this vandalism, even if he is shorthanded." She waved her hand to encompass the big plateglass window across the front of her shop.

Chase studied the *X,* which reached almost to the top of the window. He raised his hand to see if he could touch the highest point. "You know, whoever did this is either pretty tall or he used a ladder. I'm six-two, and I'd have to stretch to get paint up that high."

Holding her hair out of her face, Allison turned to look up at the offending graffiti. "Either tall, or there are two guys, one standing on the other guy's shoulders."

Chase had the feeling the vandalism was a one-culprit deal going around town making trouble just because he could. More than one troublemaker and the word would leak out. A second kid wouldn't be able to resist bragging about his extracurricular, middle-of-the-night adventures.

"Whatever." He shrugged. "I'll see if I can reach the guy we've used to wash windows. Maybe he can get over here today."

"Thanks. I'd clean it myself except business really has picked up for the holidays."

"Mine, too. That flyer with the coupon was a good idea for bringing in new customers. Which reminds me…" After yesterday morning, he wanted to avoid Viv. And Theo. It would be far too easy for him to slip right back into the old pattern with Viv, which would be neither kind nor fair to her. "Maybe you could ask Bea to bring the mail addressed to the read-a-thon over to me. That way I wouldn't have to lock up the store in the middle of the day."

"Sure. I think Bea would do that." A puzzled frown furrowed her forehead. "Is there something wrong?"

"Not at all. I just don't want to be away from the shop for any length of time. Don't want to miss a customer." Chase figured that was the phoniest line he'd ever heard and was sure Allison saw through it.

"Okay. I'll send Bea over when she delivers the mail."

"Thanks." Feeling like a heel, he walked back to his store.

"Bad birdie! Bad birdie!" Pepper squawked.

"Yeah, and I'm the worst kind of man," Chase grumbled. But he had to do whatever he could to protect Viv and Theo from the inheritance his father had passed down to him.

Bea Jorgensen, bundled up with a heavy jacket over her postal worker uniform, dropped the day's mail on the counter in the bookshop. "Since you folks started that read-a-thon business, my mailbag is getting heavier by the day."

Standing behind the counter, Vivian pulled the stack of envelopes and advertising flyers closer to her. "Yes, it's wonderful how people have reacted to the needs of the animal shelter. I checked this morning and Matt's video about the read-a-thon has more than six thousand hits now."

"Personally, I don't have the time or energy to mess with the internet. Can't think why folks spend so much time looking at a dinky little screen. They need to get out and about, like I do."

Vivian couldn't help but smile. "Then you have the perfect job, don't you?"

"I do indeed."

"Bea!" Allison hurried from the Kids' Korner to the front of the shop. "Could you do me a favor? Chase is handling the money we receive for the shelter. If I sort through this mail and give you the letters addressed to the read-a-thon, could you drop them at Fluff & Stuff?"

"I expect so," Bea said.

Vivian pressed her lips together. She kept her head and neck immobile. Disappointment stole her breath. "Isn't Chase going to come here to pick up the checks?"

"Not today." Allison quickly sorted through the mail and handed the bulk of it to Bea.

The mail carrier cheerfully held up the handful of letters in a salute. "I'm on my way. See you tomorrow, ladies."

Vivian turned to her employer. "Why isn't Chase coming here?" Her throat felt tight, her voice hoarse.

"He said he didn't want to close up his shop in the middle of the day." Allison looked directly at Vivian with a hint of sympathy in her eyes. "But I thought maybe you'd know if there was some other reason that's keeping him away."

Vivian swallowed hard. "No."

"Did you two have a fight or something? I've noticed he's been a little distant lately."

Viv heard Theo waking in the back room. "Chase came over when you were out yesterday. He told me he never intends to be a father. He doesn't want children. Ever."

Hunching her shoulders, Vivian hurried to the back room to get Theo. Her hands shook as she picked him up. Not only had Chase refused any possibility of being a father, he was letting her know in no uncertain terms that they couldn't even be friends. Not as long as she chose to be a mother.

Please, Lord, help me to accept the path You have chosen for me and celebrate the blessings You have bestowed.

Fighting tears, she hugged Theo close to her.

* * *

By Sunday, Chase was as grouchy as a bulldog with a toothache.

He missed Viv. Missed seeing her smile, hearing her voice. Missed the way his heart lifted when she came into a room.

What if I have enough faith for both of us?

That's what she'd told him, but could he believe that was possible?

He'd found families for two shelter puppies this week. Apparently people were not only sending in checks to support Happy Havens, they were adopting dogs and cats that needed a forever home. Just one puppy was left in the pen at his shop.

"Hi, little guy. Are you lonely?" He reached in to pick up the mixed brown-and-white beagle. Cute little guy.

Boyo came nosing around the pen. Chase spared a hand to reassure his dog that he was still loved.

"I'll check with Annabelle tomorrow, see if she has another couple of puppies she can loan me." Dogs liked to be part of a pack.

Truth was, so did Chase. Well, not actually a part of a pack but one half of a couple. Since he didn't want children, that didn't seem to be in his future. At least not with Viv.

I have faith in you.

You're selling yourself short.

Was he? When he thought about his father and

the cruelty that had resided in that man's heart—
assuming he had a heart—Chase couldn't under-
estimate the possibility that he had a streak of
brutality locked somewhere inside himself, too.

Faith.

Maybe the truth was he didn't have the faith that
he could give Viv and Theo what they needed.

He put the puppy back in the pen and stood.
Maybe he ought to give faith a try.

He checked his watch, saw there was plenty of
time to get to church and went upstairs to change
clothes. He couldn't remember the last time he was
inside a church. He hoped God wouldn't strike him
dead with a lightning bolt.

The drive to church was a short one, and he
pulled into a parking spot near the back. He sat
for a minute. He ran his fingers around the steering
wheel. A fleck of dirt on the dashboard attracted
his attention. He flicked it off with his fingernail.

"Come on, Chase. Either go on in or get out of
here," he said aloud. He could find other things to
do. Like go to the Red Rooster for lunch. Drive
over to the wildlife preserve to see the migrating
birds on the marshy pond.

Disgusted with himself, he pushed open the
car door, slammed it shut and headed toward the
church.

When he stepped into the vestibule, he had expected the mayor to be at this post, as Chase heard

firsthand often enough, but a man he didn't recognize handed him a program. Chase nodded his thanks.

No lightning bolt struck him down.

He eased down the side aisle. Although there were quite a few people in the church, he found an empty pew near the back and sat down.

Trying not to be conspicuous, he glanced around the church. Sun shone through a stained-glass window, dotting the congregation with color like bits of hard Christmas candy. The worship team played an up-tempo piece with trills and resounding chords that vibrated in Chase's chest. For the most part, members of the congregation sat quietly listening, some with their heads bowed in prayer or contemplation.

Chase bowed his head. *Okay, Lord, I'm here. Now what?*

He thought about Viv and how much she already loved Theo, and about his fears of being a father. He searched inside himself for a trace of the evil that had been in his father. If it was there, it was too well hidden to reveal itself easily.

But that didn't mean it wasn't there.

He clasped his hands together, staring at them as though he might discover the truth. Some assurance that he could be a decent parent, a loving husband.

The musicians finished their piece and started a new one with a dramatic flourish. Around him,

Chase heard the members of the congregation stand. He followed suit, fumbling for a hymnal stuck in a holder on the back of the pew in front of him. The pastor came out onto the stage and held up his arms as though to embrace all of those present. His baritone voice carried throughout the church as he led a hymn.

Chase had no idea what hymn they were singing, but he opened the hymnal and pretended he knew what he was doing.

When they finished singing, the congregation took their seats again, and the pastor stepped up to the pulpit.

Chase settled back to listen to the pastor welcome visitors and make announcements.

"As many of you know," the pastor said, "this evening we're serving our annual Thanksgiving dinner for the less fortunate in our community. Already we have volunteers roasting turkeys and hams, cooking potatoes and stuffing. I know personally that there are quarts of delicious homemade cranberry sauce waiting for our guests. Plus pumpkin pies by the dozen from our own Sweet Dreams Bakery. Definitely a special treat."

A ripple of laughter spread through the congregation as they realized he'd been sneaking a taste or two himself.

"We'd like to thank all of our volunteers, who will be there this afternoon to cook and serve dinner," he continued. "This has been a hard year for many of our neighbors. It's a blessing for us to share with them our bounty as our forefathers shared with those who had settled this land before them. I invite any of you who can to join us this afternoon in the Lord's work. My dear wife...Wendy Garman—" he nodded toward the woman playing the keyboard, who was so short Chase could barely see the top of her gray head "—tells me we will begin serving about four o'clock."

Chase wondered if Viv was helping with the dinner. Probably. She had a generous spirit. She and Allison and many of the residents of Bygones were unstinting when it came to helping others. Maybe that's what held a small town together in hard times: giving and sharing and caring about one another.

Chase liked being a small part of that spirit.

When the church service ended, he stood to leave. He hadn't had any great revelation, but he did feel somehow lighter, as though he had shared his burdens with someone stronger than him.

He was about to slip out the side door when he heard his name called. He turned to find Viv standing in the aisle smiling at him.

His heart did a strange little hop.

"Hi." Her cheeks were flushed and she was holding a sleeping Theo on her shoulder.

"Hi yourself."

She glanced toward the back of the church as the departing members of the congregation stopped to speak briefly with the pastor.

"I've missed seeing you lately," she said, turning back to Chase. "I guess Bea is bringing you the mail."

"Yeah, she is. We're still getting lots of checks." He'd missed seeing Viv, too. But he'd been afraid…

"I know. The thermometer keeps going up."

"I've been letting Allison know how much money has come in."

"I know." Her tongue peeked out to dampen her lips. "I'd better get Theo home. I'm helping with the dinner tonight."

"I thought you might be."

"Doing my bit, you know." A hint of sadness filled her lovely brown eyes. "Good to see you."

She turned and walked away, head held high, leaving Chase standing there feeling awkward and not very smart. Was he letting the best thing that ever happened to him simply walk out of his life?

He had the troubling sense that that was exactly what he was doing.

Chapter Twelve

Sunday afternoon, Vivian made her way through the crowded all-purpose room in the basement of the community church. Folding tables and chairs had been set out in rows. Students in Sunday-school classes had made turkeys out of their handprints, colored them and posted them on corkboards around the walls. Colorful paper tablecloths covered the tables, helping to make the room appear festive—assuming no one looked up at the rather ugly exposed pipes that ran across the ceiling.

People filled nearly every table, enjoying their early Thanksgiving dinner with all the trimmings. She knew many of them had experienced hardships during the past year.

The murmur of conversation hummed around the room, broken occasionally by a burst of laughter. Children, unable to sit still through their whole meal, darted between tables even as parents tried to corral them.

Vivian was tasked with delivering slices of pie to the guests when they were ready for dessert. In order to have both hands free, she had strapped on a fabric baby carrier in front of her, giving Theo a view of the world and the people who were eager to coo and fuss over him. Many of the women enjoying their dinners seemed more interested in Theo than a piece of pie.

"Oh, what a darling child."

"He must look just like his daddy."

Vivian didn't know if that was true or not, but he did look a lot like Chase must have as a baby, with dark hair and brown eyes. She held out the tray with slices of pie to the next woman at the table.

"Oh, honey, isn't he a doll?" Mrs. Underwood, a regular library patron, said, giving Theo a cheek pinch. "I didn't know you got married."

Vivian's cheeks heated. "Would you like some pie?" She hadn't expected so many questions about her nonexistent husband, although she should have. It seemed easier not to respond rather than trying to explain the situation to casual acquaintances.

With her tray empty, she headed back to the commercial-size kitchen adjacent to the all-purpose room to load up again. Josh Smith, who had provided the coffee for the dinner, was wearing a butcher-style apron. He stood behind a counter carving a turkey kept warm under a heat lamp. For the moment, he didn't have any customers.

"That's a pretty great way to carry a baby." His auburn hair and blue eyes almost made him look like he and Vivian were brother and sister.

"I have no idea what mothers used to do before they created all these neat things to make a mom's life easier." She rested her tray on the edge of the counter.

Josh bent to look directly at Theo. "You like riding in that thing, don't you?"

Theo jiggled up and down, waved his arms and gurgled nonsense syllables.

"I absolutely agree." Josh nodded with great seriousness. "If we'd thought of this gadget first, we would have made a fortune."

Theo blew a bubble, giggling when it popped.

Using a clean napkin, Josh wiped Theo's slobber off his chin. "Evidently you're not fond of that idea, young man. I can see we'll have to come up with a different product line."

Vivian laughed. "I'm not sure I'd be willing to take Theo's advice on inventions or investments just yet."

"Perhaps not." He tossed the napkin in the trash and smiled at Theo.

"You're good with babies," Vivian said. "Are you planning to settle down and have a family of your own?" Her question was nosy, she admitted. But she was curious about Josh. He'd revealed little of himself since he'd been in Bygones.

"Someday, I suppose." He glanced out at the crowd, scanning the room. "I have a few loose ends to tie up before I'd feel right about that."

"Oh? Like what?" Maybe like Vivian, he had a dream he had yet to fulfill.

He chuckled and started to carve more turkey as a late-arriving family of four walked up to the counter. "Well, if I was waiting to make my fortune from the Cozy Cup Café, I'd have to wait a long time, wouldn't I?"

Vivian imagined that was true, despite the fact the Cozy Cup had become a regular meeting spot for local residents, including the teens who played the computer games there. But making a fortune owning a coffee shop? She doubted that.

She could, however, easily see Josh as a family man.

She walked to the back of the kitchen where several women had sliced up pies and placed the pieces on small paper plates.

Coraline Connolly, the school principal, and Robert Randall, owner of the closed factory, were in deep conversation, standing by the large stainless steel refrigerator. Something about their body language, the way they leaned toward each other, their matching smiles, struck her as interesting. It was almost as if they were…flirting? Both of them were in their sixties. Vivian had heard a rumor that

Robert planned to leave Bygones. Yet the way they looked at each other…

Coraline's cheeks were a little flushed, although that could be a result of her helping to cook the dinner. Robert listened to her attentively, nodding often. They seemed unaware of the activity around them in the kitchen: Mrs. Andrews using a noisy giant mixer to prepare more mashed potatoes, a teenage boy Vivian didn't recognize hauling out and banging together garbage cans filled with trash.

Refilling her tray, Vivian wondered about the relationship between Coraline and Robert. Surely they'd known each other a long time. Perhaps they'd been friends, since they both lived in the community and were an important part of Bygones. Coraline was a widow, Robert a couple of years divorced.

Vivian's brows lifted with curiosity. Was it possible…?

Speculating about what Coraline and Robert might mean to each other, Vivian picked up the tray and headed out to serve those who hadn't had any pie yet. She noticed Theo had snuggled down farther in his carrier, and his head lolled to the side. "Sleepy-time boy," she whispered.

A young man who looked to be nine or ten stopped her.

"That sure is good-tasting pie," he said.

"I'm glad you like it."

He shuffled his silverware around on a plate that he'd cleared of every crumb. "I was wondering... Would it be okay for me to have a second piece?"

"Sure, I can't think why not." There were a dozen more pies yet to be cut, and the dinner crowd was beginning to thin out.

"Connor! You're not supposed to ask for seconds," his mother admonished him. "What would the pastor think?"

"Really, it's fine. Still lots of pie left." Vivian handed the boy a slice of pie. "Would you like another piece, too?" she asked his mother.

"Oh, no, I've already eaten more tonight than I did all week."

Although the woman looked to be younger than thirty, she was slightly plump. Vivian wouldn't call her overweight. Given her somewhat frayed coat, Vivian suspected she rarely had a chance to overeat.

"Do you live here in Bygones?" Vivian asked.

"We're just a bit outside of town." The woman darted her gaze around the room. "Is that all right? Is this supper just for people from Bygones?"

"Not at all. Everyone is welcome." Sensing the woman needed some help, Vivian pulled up an empty chair opposite her. "A lot of folks around here have been going through hard times lately. We're just glad we're able to share some of the

Lord's bounty with our friends and neighbors. I'm Vivian, by the way."

"Maureen. Maureen Jenkins." She fingered her empty coffee cup. "My husband—Connor's dad—passed on just over a year ago. Cancer. Things have been pretty tight for us, Connor and me. I've tried looking for a job, but there aren't many to be had, and if I found one in Wichita or Manhattan, some-place like that, I'd be leaving for work before my boy would be going to school and coming home long after dark." She shook her head. "Someone from a Save Our Streets committee said they'd put me on a list of folks looking for work. That there might be a job here in Bygones."

"That would be wonderful." Vivian wouldn't want Theo to be a latchkey child at Connor's age, which is one good reason for her to make her blog a success. "Did they say who might have a job opening?"

"They said I should talk to a Mr. Rollins? He owns the pet store?"

Vivian did a mental fist pump. She would so like for Chase to hire this woman. "I hope you like animals."

"I do," Connor blurted out, his pie plate cleaned again. "We got us two dogs and a cat. Ma says they eat too much, but I like 'em a lot."

"Good for you." Vivian focused on Maureen. "What about you?" Theo shifted his position in the carrier but didn't wake up. Vivian circled her arm around him, giving him the comfort of her closeness.

"I like animals fine, I guess. They're good company." She elbowed her son, teasing the boy. "Even if they do eat a lot just like you."

"I know the owner of the pet store, Chase Rollins. He's a very nice man. I'm sure you'd enjoy working for him."

"Truth is…" Maureen's cheeks colored, and her gaze lowered. "I'd be happy just to get a paycheck."

If Chase had been here helping with the dinner, she would have dragged him over to meet Maureen. But he wasn't here. And he probably wouldn't appreciate her dragging him anywhere.

Maureen's eyebrows rose. "You really think he might hire me?"

"I can't say for sure, but if the committee has told you so, then I'd say you have a good shot."

Suddenly Maureen's smile broke like sunshine bursting through the clouds on a spring day. "I'll drop by tomorrow while Connor's in school. We get my husband's social security, which isn't much. A part-time job close to home would make a big difference."

Vivian patted her hand. "Then I definitely hope it works out for you." She would include Maureen and her son in her prayers tonight, and she hoped to pave the way for her when she met Chase to ask for a job.

Lifting her tray, she moved on to other tables. Families chatted while they ate. Vivian delivered pie to those who wanted a slice.

Pastor Garman, who had been toiling in the kitchen under his wife's watchful eye for most of the afternoon, now stood by the wall chatting with one of the lay leaders of the church. He had long since discarded his jacket and his clerical collar.

Two pieces of pie remained on her tray. It didn't look as though there were any more takers, so Vivian strolled back into the kitchen.

"The crowd seems to be thinning out," she commented to those gathered around the serving table.

"There are still three or four pies that haven't been cut yet." Melissa, who had made and donated the pies from her bakery, frowned. "Guess it's better to have too many than too few."

Vivian had a quick thought. "I know a mother and son who'd like to take one home. The boy's a preteen and has one of those hollow legs."

Brian Montclair, who worked with Melissa at the Sweet Dreams Bakery and was now engaged to her, stepped up behind her, sliding his arm affectionately around her waist. "I was like that as a kid. My mom used to claim, for what it cost to feed me, she could have saved all the children in Africa from starvation."

Laughing, Melissa looked up fondly at her fi-ancé. "He still eats like that. Sure makes it tough to clear a profit when you have a cookie-aholic on the bakery payroll."

Helen Langston joined the crowd. The mayor's wife, who ran the family grocery store, was a tall, thin brunette who rarely smiled.

"Well, I finally did it," she announced without acknowledging she had interrupted a conversation. "I just hired a kid to work part-time afternoons at the Hometown Grocery. I'm getting so busy I don't have time to sweep up the aisles and keep the shelves straight. Of course the mayor is too swamped to help out." She sniffed as though that was a burden she had to carry on her shoulders every day of the week.

"Needing to hire an extra person sounds like business is picking up," Vivian said. "That's good news, isn't it?"

Helen narrowed her eyes. "That's what his Honor says, but it's not *his* back that's hurting." As though to emphasize the point, she walked away rubbing the small of her back.

Vivian looked at the other women standing nearby. She thought they all had a certain amount of sympathy for Helen. The woman did work hard, and she was far from young. But Vivian thought if Helen would work harder at being positive, maybe her back wouldn't hurt so much.

Melissa handed Viv one of the pies that was still in the box. "Go ahead. Maybe a whole pie will fill up that boy's leg for a few minutes, anyway."

Chuckling, Vivian went out to the widow and her son. She was sure Maureen didn't often make pies and would appreciate the treat to take home.

Thinking of Maureen and how to encourage Chase to hire the woman part-time, she recalled her mother saying the best way to a man's heart was through his stomach. A slice of fresh-baked pumpkin pie might just do the trick.

As Vivian was helping with the final cleanup, she found herself clearing a table with Coraline.

"I saw you talking with Robert earlier," she commented casually. "You were certainly deep in conversation."

"Oh, yes, I suppose we were." The faintest hint of color rose to her cheeks. "We were discussing who the town benefactor might be."

"Oh?" The conversation had looked a lot more intimate than that to Vivian. "Have you figured it out yet?"

Coraline placed dirty plates into a bin to carry into the kitchen. "I do believe I'm getting closer," she said with a secretive smile.

"Really? Who do you think it is?"

"We'll just have to wait and see, won't we?" With that, she lifted the bin of dishes and walked away.

Vivian blew out a frustrated breath. She really

would like to know the answer to that question and so would a whole lot of other folks in Bygones.

Sometime later, Vivian put her sleepy baby boy in his car seat and a wrapped slice of pie in the passenger seat, and drove into town. Main Street was deserted on a Sunday evening. Only security lights shone through the recently cleaned downstairs shop windows, although Chase's lights were visible in his second-floor apartment above his store.

She parked the car in front of Fluff & Stuff but didn't plan to go inside. Just a quick stop to deliver the pie and tell Chase about Maureen.

"Touchdown! Touchdown!" In his cage in Chase's upstairs apartment, Pepper squawked and shook his string of shiny bells.

Sunday night football on TV wasn't holding Chase's attention, and Pepper's running commentary wasn't helping. Sitting in a recliner in his minuscule living room, he had his shoes off and his feet propped up. Fluff lay curled in his lap, Boyo beside his chair. The consummate domestic scene in a bachelor's life.

Idly he ran his fingers through Fluff's thick coat and scratched the top of her head.

Maybe he should have volunteered to help at the church's Thanksgiving dinner.

But he would have felt self-conscious. Out of place. They probably had plenty of volunteers anyway.

He would have been able to see Vivian.

He didn't want her to think he was stalking her.

Because he wasn't. He was trying to keep his distance.

And not doing very well at it.

Boyo came to his feet at the same moment Chase heard the buzzer sound on the front door of the shop downstairs. From Pepper's perch by the window, he squawked, "What's up? What's up?"

Who would be calling on him on a Sunday evening?

Boyo went to the door of the apartment and stood, waiting expectantly for Chase to open it.

Easing Fluff off his lap, Chase slid his feet into his shoes. He didn't bother to tie the laces. It was probably some kid going along the street playing ding-dong-ditch-'em on everybody's doorbell.

He trotted down the stairs behind Boyo, whose tail was wagging like crazy. Apparently the caller wasn't a stranger. The security light near the cash register lit the shop, leaving much of it in shadow.

Before he reached the ground floor, he spotted Vivian at the door. She smiled and waved at him.

His rate of descent down the last couple of steps accelerated and so did his heartbeat. He hurried across the shop, easily making his way around displays. Unlocking the door, he pulled it open.

His breath lodged in his lungs.

She stood in front of him looking beautiful, her

coat pulled snugly around her, her auburn hair slightly mussed, her blue eyes sparkling in the dim light. Her cheeks were rosy in the chill night air.

Boyo brushed past him, demanding attention from their caller.

"Hey," he said as a greeting. *Smooth, Rollins. Real smooth.*

"Hey yourself." She bent to give Boyo a pat.

Gathering himself, trying not to appear too socially inept, he opened the door wider. "Come on in out of the cold."

"I can't stay."

His hopes, the wild thoughts that had spun through his imagination, deflated like a blow-up Christmas decoration in somebody's front yard.

"I brought you a slice of pie from the church dinner." She handed him the paper plate. "We had lots of pies left over."

"Oh, well, thanks. That was very thoughtful of you." He'd have liked it even better if she'd come by to talk, to have coffee with him. *But you effectively told her to get lost. Make up your mind, Rollins.*

"Actually, it was an excuse to talk to you for a moment." Her smile held an invitation.

His spirits perked up. "You sure you don't want to come in?" They could go upstairs. Share the pie. Talk about lots of things—the read-a-thon, the Happy Havens shelter...

"I can't. Theo's in the car. I need to get him home."

"Oh. Okay." It finally registered that the lights on Viv's car were still on, the engine running. She hadn't planned to stay at all.

"I talked to a woman at the dinner. Maureen Jenkins. Apparently she and her son have been having hard times lately. Her husband passed away a little over a year ago. The Save Our Streets committee put her on a list of prospective employees from the local area."

Chase nodded to acknowledge what she said, even though he didn't know where she was going with this information.

"She said she'd been given your name as someone who might be hiring some part-time help."

His forehead tightened. "Yeah, that's true. I haven't quite decided, but they did mention—"

"Well, she may stop by to talk with you sometime this week. She seemed very nice. She really does need a job. As a favor to me, I'd really appreciate it if you'd at least talk to her."

"Okay. I'd be happy to talk to her." How could he deny Viv any favor?

"Great." She stepped forward, stood on tiptoes and kissed Chase on the cheek. "Thanks. I knew you'd understand."

With that, she scurried to her car, waved and backed out of the parking spot.

Stunned, Chase watched her drive down the street. He had to suppress the urge to run after her.

Gooseflesh rose on his arms. "Come on, Boyo. Let's get inside where it's warm."

He grinned as he went up the stairs. A kiss on the cheek was a nice reward for talking to a friend of Viv's about a possible job.

At dawn the next morning, Pepper started to shriek. Barking, Boyo scrambled from the foot of the bed where he'd been sleeping and raced into the living room.

Chase blinked his eyes open. "What are you guys up to?"

He struggled out of bed in his sleep pants and T-shirt, stuffed his feet in his slippers and grabbed his flannel robe. Pepper almost never squawked when his cage was covered. Boyo rarely barked at anything.

Chase sniffed the air, half expecting to smell smoke. He couldn't imagine why else the two of them would be carrying on so. But he didn't catch any scent that warned of danger.

He checked out the front apartment window that overlooked Main Street. Nothing moved there at all, and no flames licked from the tops of the old buildings that he could see.

Could someone have broken into his shop? If so, Pepper was one sharp watch-bird.

Tucking his cell phone into his pocket, he went

downstairs. Everything in the store looked normal. No one around.

Upstairs, Pepper kept up his racket.

His tail lowered, Boyo made a beeline for the back door.

"Okay, fella, let's see what's going on out there." The moment Chase opened the door, Boyo raced to the back gate, which was always shut unless the pet store was receiving a delivery.

Boyo sat staring at the gate. A low growl rumbled in his chest.

Not knowing what was on the other side of the wood gate, Chase moved cautiously. He unlatched the gate and opened it a crack.

Nothing. No one leaped in to attack him. No wild dogs or escaped circus animals on the prowl.

As he opened the gate farther, Boyo squeezed through, barking like crazy. He turned hard down the alley, his feet sliding on the loose gravel.

When the gate was fully open, Chase spotted the problem. Graffiti!

The vandal had gotten him again!

Anger and frustration rose in his chest. He clenched his jaw. Rage simmered in his gut.

Down the alley, Chase spotted Boyo speeding after the figure of a man and gaining on him. The guy tossed something into a garbage can as he ran by.

Grabbing his phone from the pocket of his robe,

Chase punched in 9-1-1 and ran in pursuit of the vandal. The hem of his robe flapped against his legs. This time the kid wasn't going to get away. The whole town was tired of him messing with them. This was a good town. With good people. They didn't deserve this.

Chase was going to bring him down.

"This is 9-1-1. What is your emergency?" the female dispatcher asked.

"I'm in the alley behind the new shops." Chase gasped for more air. "I'm in pursuit of the vandal. Get Chief Sheridan over here in a hurry."

Whoever he was chasing, the guy had long legs and a lot more wind than Chase did.

"I've notified the chief," the dispatcher said. "Can you describe the vandal? What he's wearing?"

"Red jacket with a hood. Jeans." Chase's slippers pounded on the hard asphalt. "He's almost to Bronson."

Boyo had caught up with the guy, and was barking and nipping at his heels.

The guy turned. He tried to shake off the dog.

Chase got a quick look at his face. Young. A teenager who looked vaguely familiar and was in big trouble.

"Stop!" he shouted.

"Leave me alone. I haven't hurt anybody," the kid shouted back.

When he got close enough, Chase dived at the

young man. They crashed together onto the sidewalk in a tumble of arms and legs. The boy shouted, "Get off of me! I didn't do nothin'!"

Chase felt the burn of concrete scraping his knees through his sleep pants. He was getting too old for this.

Chapter Thirteen

Joe Sheridan picked up the teenager by the back of his jacket and held him against the wall of the building. The kid was a couple of inches taller than Joe but not nearly as muscular.

Still on guard duty, Boyo snarled at the kid.

"You all right, Chase?" the chief asked. His patrol car was parked at a blocking angle at the corner, its lights still flashing.

Chase staggered to his feet, then bent over with his hands on his knees. "I will be…as soon as I can catch my breath." And get some antiseptic on his scrapes. They stung like crazy. Which probably made him equally crazy for having gone after the vandal on his own. After all, the kid could have had a weapon on him.

Joe, a former marine in his forties, chuckled. He looked formidable in his leather jacket with a By-gones Police logo shoulder patch and a blue baseball cap with a matching insignia. Chase wouldn't want to cross him.

"Remind me to send you a copy of my conditioning program. Can't have you civilians running out of gas before you catch a suspect. Particularly since the department's shorthanded."

Chase doubted he could keep up with the workout regime Joe followed so rigorously. But Chase ought to do something about getting into shape.

Snapping handcuffs on the boy, Joe turned him around, and looked him up and down, a puzzled expression on his face. "Rory? You're Liston's boy, aren't you?".

Rory slid his gaze over to Chase, then lowered his eyes. "Yes, sir. And you laid him off," the boy mumbled.

"On the high school basketball team, right?"

"Yes, sir," he responded in a glum voice that matched his expression.

"So why were you running?" Joe asked.

"That guy and his dog were chasing me. What was I supposed to do?" The kid's bravado sounded forced.

"I was chasing you because you'd done a graffiti number on my back fence. Just like you'd done to my shop window." Still steaming, Chase had to work at holding his temper.

"You can't prove that," Rory said, a stubborn set to his jaw.

"Yeah, I can." Chase pointed an accusing finger at the young man. "You've got red paint all over your hands. And I saw you throw the spray can in the trash a few buildings down from mine." He turned to Joe. "He tossed it in the bin behind the flower shop."

"I'll check it out. You did good, Chase." He frowned. "Not so sure about what you're wearing, though. Hard to scare a perp in your pajamas."

Chase hitched up his pants. His ankles were on display. They hadn't seen the sun in many years and were as white as those of an albino chimpanzee.

"I left my place in kind of a hurry," Chase said.

Joe's lips quirked. "I guessed that." He hooked his arm through Rory's. "Come on, son. You're going to spend a little time sitting in a cell while I give your dad a call."

"Leave him out of it, okay?" the boy mumbled as he was escorted to Joe's police car.

A few vehicles had passed on the street, slowing to see what was going on. Chase decided that meant he should make a quick retreat to his own place if he didn't want his unfashionable morning attire to be the subject of the town gossip.

"Come on, Boyo. You've done your duty, now let's get on home before the whole town starts talking."

Car tires squealed.

Chase looked up in time to see Viv flying out

of her car, leaving the door open and racing toward him.

"What happened? Are you all right? I was coming to work early to do some paperwork, and I saw the chief's car, and then I saw you...." Her voice broke. Her cheeks were bright red from either the chill morning air or excitement. She'd never looked more beautiful.

Backpedaling, Chase tried to wave her off. "I'm fine. The police chief just caught our vandal."

"Chase is the hero," Joe called out before he slammed the squad car door on Rory. "He's the one who caught our guy."

Viv's eyes widened. "You did? How? Are you sure you're not hurt?"

He took a few more steps backward. "A few scrapes. No big deal."

Her gaze scanned his knees. Her cheeks turned pale. "You're bleeding."

"I am?" He looked down. Sure enough. One knee was oozing a little blood through a rip in his sleep pants where he'd banged it across the concrete while tackling Rory. "It's nothing. I'll take care of it when I get home." He began walking back to his place.

"Not alone, you won't."

Before he knew what was happening, Viv hurried back to her car and was driving down the alley beside him. "Do you want a ride? I'll drive you."

"It's not very far, Viv." Embarrassed, he picked up his pace. He didn't want his friends and neighbors to poke their heads out the window and see Viv escorting him back to his shop in his robe.

There was no stopping her. When he turned in through the open service gate, she was right behind him in her car.

"I've got a first-aid kit in the car. Do you want me to bring it in?" she asked.

"No, I've got some stuff upstairs." If he could manage to get inside the shop—

"I have to get Theo, and then I'll be right there. Don't do anything until I can sterilize the wound."

He glanced over his shoulder. She was the most persistent Florence Nightingale he'd ever met. She was planning to storm right up to his apartment and nurse him right there. The place was a mess. He hadn't put away the dinner dishes. Several months' worth of *Animal Life* magazines were scattered around the living room.

And he was in his pajamas.

"On second thought," he said. "Bring the first-aid kit. You can doctor me on the loading dock."

She peered up over her car door. "You sure? Theo won't be a problem. I can carry him—"

He sat down on the edge of the cold loading dock and covered himself as best he could with his robe. "Here will be fine."

* * *

"How did you know the vandal was around?" she asked as she crouched next to Chase to quickly apply antiseptic to his scrapes.

Boyo had parked himself on the other side of Chase, his ears alert and tail wagging as though he was waiting to race off after another culprit.

"Pepper woke me up right about dawn. He never—" He drew a sharp breath as she dabbed the stinging antiseptic on the deepest cut on his knee.

"Sorry," she whispered.

"No problem. Anyway, Pepper's squawking woke me up. At first I thought he must have smelled smoke or something like that. He rarely makes any noise until I take the cover off his cage in the morning."

She lifted her gaze to meet his. "So it was like Pepper knew there was trouble? He thought you were in danger and was protecting you?"

Chase's brows pulled together. "I guess you could say that."

"Pretty smart bird, huh?"

"Yeah, he is." He seemed to ponder that though for a moment before continuing. "His racket woke up Boyo, too." Idly, he petted the dog. "When Boyo and I came downstairs, he ran right to the back gate and waited until I opened it. Then he took off after that kid. I followed them."

"That was very brave of you. Chief Sherida

ought to give you a medal." She'd been so scared when she'd seen the flashing police lights and then Chase with the police chief. Afraid that he'd been seriously hurt. Or something bad had happened at the pet shop.

Chase shrugged off her suggestion of a medal. "What I did qualifies for stupidity, not bravery. I didn't want the kid to get away. I was tired of him messing with the town and people like Amos Mahnken, who have to undo what he does. Assuming the kid pulled down the fence like I suspect."

Vivian turned her attention to applying the bandage. "You could have been seriously hurt if the fellow you were chasing had had a weapon."

"All he had was a spray can, which he ditched behind Love in Bloom."

"Was that Rory Liston I saw the chief putting in his squad car?" she asked.

"That's what he said his name was. He looked familiar, but I didn't know his name."

"That's a real shame and a surprise, too. Rory is one of the kids in Allison's after-school creative writing class. He's on Sam's basketball team at school. They'll both be very disappointed in him."

"I figured he might play basketball. Tall kid."

She puzzled over Rory's arrest. The young man had always seemed so polite. She never would have suspected he was the vandal who had been plaguing the town.

Vivian heard Theo fussing in the car.

"Hang on a minute. I've got to get Theo out of his car seat."

Chase stood when she did. "I can take care of the other knee."

She gave him a gentle shove in the middle of his chest, forcing him to sit down again. "Stay put. I'll be right back."

She returned quickly and handed Theo to Chase. "You'll have to hold him while I clean the road rash on your other knee."

For an instant, Chase resisted taking Theo, and then he succumbed to the baby's nonsensical verbal entreaty.

Theo quieted his fussing the moment Chase settled the baby in his lap. "Hey, big guy. You're up early, aren't you?"

Theo's little hand reached up to grab Chase's chin. He nibbled the baby's fingers, which made Theo laugh.

Sitting back on her heels, Vivian watched their interaction. Theo was totally fascinated by Chase. He patted Chase's whiskered cheek, stuck his tiny fingers in Chase's mouth, and finally plucked at the dark chest hair that peeked out above Chase's T-shirt.

"Easy, kiddo. That hair's attached." With great gentleness, Chase released the baby's grip.

Tears swam in Vivian's eyes. The two of them

were so beautiful together, so obviously enamored of one another, it was impossible that Chase believed he might hurt a child. Ever. It simply wasn't a part of his character.

There had to be another reason Chase was holding back.

When Viv finally finished nursing Chase's skinned knees, he sent her and Theo on to the bookstore to work and escaped upstairs to his apartment.

Her gentle touch had astounded him. He couldn't recall the last time a woman had cared for him in that way. Not since he'd been little and his mother had kissed his boo-boos to make them all better.

With her seated before him, her caress so gentle and feminine, it was all he could do to keep from kissing her. Holding her in his arms.

He shut the apartment door behind him and tossed his bathrobe on the couch. His hands trembled as he lifted the cover from Pepper's cage.

"Bad birdie! Bad birdie!" Pepper jumped up and down on his perch making the whole cage rock.

"You're a good birdie, Pepper. Next ad I place in the newspaper, I'm going to call you an excellent watch-bird."

Boyo whined.

"Yeah. You, too, Boyo."

Fluff trotted out from the bedroom and jumped up on top of the TV.

"Sorry, Fluff. No watch-cat points for you. Sleeping through the entire incident doesn't count."

That news didn't appear to bother Fluff.

He grabbed a cracker for Pepper and slipped it to the bird. The parrot deserved a medal. Without Pepper's wake-up call, Chase never would have caught the vandal. Instead he'd be calling a painter to cover the graffiti not only on his gate but probably on a half dozen other gates down the alley.

Maybe he ought to think twice about selling Pepper.

He opened the cage. Pepper hopped onto his hand, then walked up his arm to perch on his shoulder.

"Good birdie," Pepper crooned and pressed his head against Chase's.

The tickle of Pepper's feathers made Chase smile, pretty much the same way Theo's tiny slobbery hand grabbing his chin caught him off guard, and he found himself liking it.

Baby Theo didn't seem to care about the scar on his chin. It was just something new to explore with his little fingers.

After all these years, maybe that's how Chase ought to think about his scar. Not a symbol of the angry man who had beaten him. But just a part of Chase's history that no longer mattered.

Just maybe he'd outgrown that snapshot of his father as a boy and become a man on his own.

But how could he be sure?

Letting Pepper ride on his shoulder, he went into the bathroom to find some antiseptic for the scrape on his elbow. At least Viv hadn't known about that minor injury. Chase had had about all the sweet doctoring he could handle for one day.

Pepper peered into the mirror over the sink and flapped his wings. "Pretty birdie! Pretty birdie!"

Chase laughed. "Definitely a pretty birdie."

Early that afternoon a woman walked into the pet shop and glanced around as if looking for something in particular.

"What's up? What's up?" Pepper greeted her.

Chase, who was stacking bags of cat food, spotted her, although he didn't recognize her. "Hi there. Can I help you find something?" he asked. Probably in her thirties, she wore a tailored blouse and skirt with low heels.

"I'm looking for Mr. Rollins, the owner?" she asked in a tentative voice.

"You've found him." He brushed the dust off his hands and walked to the front of the shop. "What can I do for you?"

Pepper squawked again, and she sent the bird a shy smile before turning back to Chase.

"My name's Maureen Jenkins." She fussed with the handle of her small purse. "The people from Save Our Streets said you might have a job opening. And yesterday at the church Thanksgiving dinner, I talked to Vivian Duncan. Such a sweet young woman. She thought you might be looking to hire someone part-time." A faint trace of hope sparked in her nutmeg eyes.

Chase had to give the woman credit. She hadn't wasted any time coming in to apply for the job.

"Viv mentioned you might come by." His business had been picking up lately, particularly since the discount flyer had been distributed to neighboring towns. With Christmas approaching, he hoped his sales would grow even more. "Tell me about where you've worked before."

"I'm afraid I've had only one job, and it was a long time ago. I did cashiering and stocking at a Circle K."

"Okay. Did you like doing that?"

A smile blossomed unexpectedly. "I loved having the customers come in, especially the regulars who stopped for coffee and whatnot. I began thinking of them as friends."

"Come again. Come again." Pepper banged his beak against the wire cage.

Maureen sent Pepper a curious look. "Does he always talk like that?"

"Pretty much. Does that bother you?"

"No, not at all. I'm just amazed." She shrugged. "I've never been around a parrot before."

"His name's Pepper. There's a grape on the counter. Would you like to feed him one?"

"Oh, yes, could I?" She eagerly picked up the grape and held it out to the bird. "Hello, Pepper. I'm Maureen. You must be the smartest bird in the whole world. And so pretty."

Pepper puffed up his chest and fluttered his wings before reaching delicately for the grape. He cooed softly. "Pretty birdie."

"Mrs. Jenkins, I do believe Pepper likes you, and he's a very good judge of character. You're hired." Of course, the fact that Viv had recommended the woman added some weight to Chase's decision.

She gasped. "Really?"

"Really." Her excitement and evident relief pleased Chase. She'd do just fine. "Let me have you fill out a form to get all your information. If it's all right with you, I'd like you to start the Friday after Thanksgiving. All the shops in Bygones will be having sales, and we're hoping to draw a big crowd for Black Friday."

"That sounds wonderful."

"We'll work out later how many hours a week make sense based on the traffic we get. I can't guarantee anything after Christmas, but I'm sure I can use you through the holidays." He named an hourly rate, which seemed to suit her.

"Thank you so much, Mr. Rollins. I can't tell you how much this means to me."

"Call me Chase. Everyone does. And if I may, I'll call you Maureen."

She flushed slightly. "Of course."

They went over some of the details of the job. Maureen grasped everything readily including how to use the cash register. When she left the store, Pepper sent her on the way with a cheerful, "Come again. Come again."

"I will, Pepper. I promise."

As Maureen closed the door and walked down the sidewalk, Chase grinned to himself. "You're coming up in the world, Rollins. You just hired your very first employee."

Vivian was surprised later that afternoon when Sam arrived at Happy Endings, Nicky and Rosie in tow.

"Hey, Sam, no basketball practice this afternoon?" she asked.

Grimacing, he rolled his eyes. "My assistant took over while I spent my time dealing with our star basketball forward at the police department."

"Oh, you must be talking about Rory Liston, right?" It pained Vivian to know a boy with such a good future had turned to vandalism. "I can't imagine what got into him."

Rosie spotted Allison and ran to the Kids' Korner to greet her, raising her arms to be picked up.

"Look at you, Rosie-Roo." Allison hefted the three-year-old into her arms, carrying her toward her daddy. "All done with preschool for today?"

"Daddy came and got us."

"Yes. So I see." Allison stretched up on tiptoe to give Sam a kiss. "I'm guessing you've been dealing with Rory Liston's problem. Viv told me about the incident this morning."

"I have spent most of the afternoon with Joe Sheridan along with Rory and his parents. That kid has really gotten himself in deep trouble. At least the police chief agreed to let Rory go in his parents' custody."

Nicky came around behind the counter and climbed up on the stool beside Vivian.

"Be careful, honey," she warned the boy, placing a steadying hand on his back. He reached for a pen and a piece of paper on the counter.

"So how did Rory's parents react to his vandalism?" Allison asked.

"Disappointed. Rory kept saying he'd done the vandalism for his father. He thought if the crime rate went up, that Joe would have to rehire his dad." Sam unzipped his jacket, revealing a Bygones High School T-shirt.

Vivian could certainly sympathize with the boy's situation: one more tragic outcome from the closing of the factory.

The bookstore door opened again and in walked Chase wearing his chinos and a long-sleeve polo shirt.

A flutter of pleasure wove its way around Vivian's heart, and she smiled.

Chase stopped abruptly just inside the door. "Wow. I didn't know there was a party going on."

"Not exactly a party," Sam said. "I came looking for advice about Rory Liston from the wise woman in my life."

"I'm afraid I'm the one who caught Rory red-handed. Literally," Chase admitted.

Allison let Rosie slide down to the floor. The little girl headed right back to the Kids' Korner, no doubt to find her favorite book.

"I'm not sure I have any advice for you, Sam. Sounds to me like the boy was trying to solve a problem that's way over his head. Maybe he could use some counseling to help him through this hard time."

"If they could afford it," Sam said. "His dad's been out of work since the summer. Money's tight. That's hard on a family. I'm just glad the boy was caught—thanks to you, Chase—before he slid into anything more dangerous than graffiti and knocking over a few picnic tables at The Everything."

"I hope getting arrested will scare him straight and teach him a lesson," Chase said.

"Me, too," Sam agreed. "He's a really good kid. Just mixed up."

Nicky asked for more paper by pointing and saying, "More."

Allison handed him a scratch pad to scribble on.

"Chase, did you come over for something special?" she asked.

He gave her a lopsided grin. "Two things, actually."

"I hope they're good things," Allison said. "Having his star player arrested hasn't made for a good day for Sam."

"They are good. Better than good. First, I tallied up the donations to Happy Havens this morning." He handed Allison a ledger sheet with the summary of receipts. "We've topped sixty-five-hundred dollars."

"My goodness! We're more than halfway to our goal." Allison's hand flew to her chest. "I never really expected—"

"That's wonderful, Chase." Filled with joy, Vivian slipped past Nicky and held up her hand to give Chase a high five. He came closer, caught her fingers between his and held on. A ripple of awareness, the heated memory of nursing his scrapes, sped down her arm to lodge in her chest. "I'm so glad for you and Annabelle and all the animals."

"You're the one who really organized the read-a-thon," he reminded her without releasing her hand.

"I'd say we've all done it together," Allison said. "And we really owe much of the success to Matt and his YouTube video."

"I'll send him another email to let him know how well it's going," Vivian volunteered. She looked at Chase and reluctantly withdrew her hand. "You said two things?"

"Right." He stuck his thumbs in the corner of his front pockets and rocked back on his heels. "You are looking at the proud employer of one part-time employee. Maureen Jenkins."

"You hired her?" Vivian cried.

"She starts Friday. The day after Thanksgiving."

"I'm so happy for her." Vivian leaped up to wrap her arms around Chase's neck and hug him. "And for you. Thank you. Thank you."

Chase, shifting their positions slightly, hugged her back. Vivian felt herself melting against him. Catching the scent of his shaving lotion. Wanting the happily ever after she'd only read about in books and didn't dare dream would come true.

"Hey, hey." Sam laughed. "Children present. Easy does it, you two."

Chase released Vivian, and she instantly missed the strength and warmth of his arms around her.

"Sorry." Heat flooded her cheeks. She hadn't meant to make a scene. But she'd been so happy for Maureen, who really needed the job. And so grateful to Chase for hiring her.

Still chuckling, Sam came around the counter to lift Nicky into his arms.

"Come on, buddy. That's enough writing for now. You can finish your novel later. Let us and Rosie get on home and start dinner. With a little good timing, Allison will join us for dinner, and it will be ready when she gets there."

"Sounds like a wonderful idea to me," Allison said, her eyes glowing with happiness and love. "I'll be there in an hour or so."

"Speaking of dinners, Chase," Vivian said. "My mother wanted me to make sure that all the new shopkeepers in town had a place to go for Thanksgiving dinner. You're invited if you're interested. We usually eat around three."

Chewing on his lip, he held her gaze for a moment. "I, um, don't know. I haven't thought that far—"

"It's okay." She masked her hurt with a bright smile. "Just know there's always room for one more at the Duncan table."

Sam said goodbye, and he and his children were going out the door when Vivian's cell phone vibrated. She pulled it from her pocket and checked the caller.

Jackie at the adoption agency.

Walking into the back room to take the call, Vivian held her breath, hoping and praying that it wasn't bad news.

Chapter Fourteen

Chase noticed Viv's worried look as she went to the back room to take the phone call. He'd hang around for a few minutes. There might be a problem with her folks. Or a sibling. With six kids in the family, one or the other probably had a crisis regularly.

Or maybe the call was about Theo.

Chase didn't like the thought of that.

"Is there something else you wanted?" Allison asked. With Sam and the twins gone, it was just the two of them in the bookstore now.

"Hmm, no, not really. Maybe I'll browse around for a book." He wasn't much of a reader. But maybe he should be. If he found a good book to read, he and Viv could talk about it. That would be something nice to share over a cup of coffee some morning. Or maybe over lunch at the Red Rooster. Except they wouldn't be having lunch together again. Or coffee. Because Chase had told her in no uncertain terms that that was the way he wanted it.

"Take as much time as you need," Allison said. "If you have any questions, I'd be happy to answer them."

"Thanks." He found the mystery section and picked up a book at random. He knew nothing about authors. He did watch a few mysteries on TV and late-night crime shows.

He sensed more than heard Viv return to the front of the store.

Glancing around, he saw she had Theo in her arms. Her beautiful blue eyes swam with tears.

In two steps he was beside her, one hand on her shoulder, the other caressing Theo's back. "What's wrong?"

Her chin trembled. "That was…the adoption agency."

Allison, apparently realizing there was a problem, came closer. "Is there something wrong with Theo?"

"No." Viv drew a shaky breath. She blinked, squeezing out a single tear.

"What is it, Viv?" Chase brushed back a few strands of hair that had fallen across her face. His stomach clenched. What had happened? Did the fool agency tell her she wouldn't do as a mother?

"A relative…Theo's aunt." Vivian hiccupped.

"She's thinking about adopting him." She placed Theo's head against her shoulder and held him tight.

"They wouldn't give Theo to this aunt, would they?" Allison sputtered. "I mean, where has she been for the past four or five months? If she was so anxious to adopt Theo, why hadn't she said something ages ago?"

"Is that what's happening?" Chase wasn't sure if Viv would survive giving up Theo. It would break her heart.

"It may be." Viv carried Theo over to a reading chair in the corner and sat down. Her grip on the baby was so strong, he started to squirm.

"They can't do that!" Allison insisted. "It's crazy. I know you said it was a possibility. But you've bonded with Theo, and now they want to take him away from you and give him to a complete stranger? Nonsense."

Chase tended to agree but he didn't get a vote. "Viv told me when she got Theo that it might be temporary. That if a relative decided to—"

"Don't you dare say I told you so," Viv snapped, glaring up at him.

He took a step back. "I didn't mean—"

"You warned me not to get too attached. Well, that's just too bad because I am attached, and I can't undo that. Not now. Not ever. I love him too much." Her chin wobbled and another big fat tear edged down her cheek.

Feeling helpless, Chase stood there like a dunce. He didn't know what to say or do, and didn't think Viv wanted him there at all. He had been afraid this would happen. That Viv would be hurt if she cared too much. Now it looked like his fears were coming true.

More times than not, dreams didn't come true. Like his mother never getting a chance for a promotion. Or a big raise. Or Chase not going to college because he had to help his mom pay the bills.

He was so sorry Viv had to learn about disappointment the hard way.

Allison knelt next to Viv. "Let's take this one step at a time. What exactly did the agency person say?"

Viv adjusted Theo to a more comfortable position and gave him a rattle to play with. "She said the aunt was considering adopting him."

"So it isn't a done deal?"

"Not yet." Viv lifted her head, her eyes red-rimmed. "I had so many plans for Theo's first Christmas. And now…"

"I'm sorry, Viv," Chase said.

She didn't seem to hear or care about his apology, and he felt a fissure open in his heart. A painful rupture he hadn't experienced before.

"So how soon is this aunt going to decide?" Allison asked.

"I don't know." Viv wiped her eyes with the back of her hand. "Whenever she does, she'll have priority over me. She can be Theo's mother just by saying she wants him."

"I'm sure she'll have to go through a screening process," Allison said.

Pulling a clean tissue from his pocket, Chase handed it to Viv. She barely nodded in acknowledgment.

Allison smoothed her hand over Viv's hair. "Well, I for one don't think you should give up on Theo yet. Since this woman didn't come forward until now, I'm not convinced she's serious about adopting Theo."

Chase figured Allison was trying to give Viv some hope. He wasn't sure that was the right thing to do. Adoption agencies no doubt had their rules, and it wouldn't be easy to get them to change their minds.

"Do you really think the aunt will decide not to adopt him?" Viv asked.

Her plea came from some reservoir of hope and faith that Chase had never had. He wasn't confident it was real and would be afraid to count on it.

"I don't know what will happen," Allison admitted. "Why don't we pray and put it in God's hands?"

The two women put their heads together, and Allison began to pray for guidance and the Lord's help.

Chase didn't have an up-close-and-personal relationship with God. And he sure didn't pray often. But he closed his eyes, bowed his head and joined his silent prayer with theirs.

Maybe God would be so surprised to find Chase praying for the second time in a week that He'd listen and grant Viv her deepest wish: to be Theo's forever mother.

Somehow Vivian managed to drive home after work without running off the road. Her whole body had been shaking since the phone call from Jackie.

Jackie had been kind, of course. And tried to tell her to relax, that nothing would change with Theo immediately. But Jackie did feel obligated to warn Vivian that Theo's aunt had inquired about adoption. Jackie and her staff would be interviewing the aunt this week and checking her background.

And then what? Would that take days? Or weeks?

Vivian couldn't bear to think what might happen next.

At home she fed Theo a bottle and held him for a long time. Her cell phone sat on one of the red garden stools she used as a coffee table. A part of her wanted to smash the phone into tiny bits, pick up Theo and run as far away from Bygones as she could. Vanish into the crowds of a big city. Or hide out in Tahiti.

None of that was possible.

She'd known from the start that she might lose Theo. That a relative might decide to adopt him. That she might have to hand him to another woman to hold and love and raise.

But the instant love she'd felt for Theo hadn't allowed her to even consider that possibility. She'd been in denial.

Now the reality had slammed into her like a summer tornado. Her whole life seemed out of kilter. The balance she'd tried to achieve had slipped away, replaced by fear and despair.

If only...

A knock on the door startled her.

Her very first thought was that Chase had come to comfort her. That he would hold her in his arms and tell her everything would be all right. That he'd be the strong one to see her through this nightmare.

But when she looked through the side window, she saw the figure of her mother silhouetted by the front porch light.

She swallowed the bitter taste of disappointment. Chase had made it clear he didn't want to be a father. She couldn't count on him to understand how much the thought of losing Theo hurt. How it burned a hole deep inside her that would never be filled again.

Carrying the sleeping baby in her arms, she opened the front door.

"Hi, honey." Her mother, dressed in her warm coat, smiled brightly. "I was coming home from Mildred Farnsworth's house. Her daughter is having a baby, and she gave her a baby shower. I saw your light on..."

Vivian lost what little control of her emotions she'd managed to hold on to since the phone call. She wept the tears that hadn't yet fallen.

"Mom," she wailed. "I may lose Theo."

Chase had worried all night about Viv, and how she was coping with the news about Theo. He had tried to think of something he could do to help her, and he'd come up empty.

He hefted Pepper's cage from its spot in his living room. "Come on, big guy. Time to open up the shop and meet the crowds that await us."

"What's up? What's up?" Pepper clung to his perch as Chase carried him downstairs.

He glanced behind him to be sure Boyo was coming, too. Couldn't run a pet store without his feathered and furry friends, he thought, as Fluff shot past him ahead of them all. His small menagerie of friends.

Shortly after Chase switched the sign on the front

door from Closed to Open, a man who looked to be in his fifties strolled into the store.

"What's up? What's up?" Pepper greeted the gentleman.

"Good morning," Chase called from the puppy pen, where he had been giving them fresh water. The video to publicize the financial need of Happy Havens had also attracted potential owners for several puppies, and he had borrowed more from the shelter to show off in the shop. "I'll be right with you."

"No rush," the customer responded.

Boyo left Chase's side to perform his welcoming duties at the front of the store.

Chase gave the pair of poodle-terrier mix puppies one last pat then strolled up to the front counter. "How can I help you?"

"I'm Stuart Peckam. I called a few days ago about the parrot you have for sale. Guess this is him, huh?"

"Oh, right." Chase had almost forgotten about that phone call. Now he felt a moment of...panic? Which was ridiculous. The whole idea of taking in Pepper was to sell him for a profit. "His name is Pepper. He's a green-cheeked Amazon. You can tell by the red topknot. Pretty rare bird."

"Pretty birdie. Pretty birdie," Pepper announced, hopping around on the floor of his cage.

"Does he talk a lot?" Stuart asked.

"When he gets rolling, it's like a monologue. You can't shut him up," Chase told him with a certain amount of pride, like a parent might brag that his child was good at arithmetic.

Avoiding Boyo, who was sitting right in front of him, Stuart walked around the cage peering at Pepper. The parrot kept his beady eyes on the stranger, mimicking the man's movements, following his every gesture.

"The thing is, since our kids moved out, my wife gets lonely in the house all day with no one to talk to. I was thinking a parrot might help her to not be so lonely."

Pepper squawked. "Polly's not here. Polly's not here."

"I imagine having a parrot would help." Although Chase thought it might be better if his wife got out of the house more and interacted with actual people.

"Tomorrow's her birthday. I thought I'd surprise her."

Chase sensed a red flag. "I don't know about surprising her with a parrot. Maybe she ought to come into the shop to meet Pepper first. Unless getting a parrot is her idea." Not every Tom, Dick or Mary cared for big birds.

"Good birdie," Pepper crooned, weaving his head back and forth.

"Well, she's allergic to cats. Besides, cats just

sort of lay around, so a cat wouldn't be much company for her."

"How about a puppy? I've got a couple of cute little guys from the shelter available for adoption." Why he was trying to talk this man out of buying a six-hundred-dollar parrot was beyond him.

"No, I like the parrot. He's got personality." He stuck his finger into the cage.

Pepper bit him.

"Ouch!" The guy yanked his hand back in a hurry and stared at the drop of blood on his fingertip.

Chase grimaced. "Sorry about that. If you decide to buy Pepper, I'll toss in a book about handling and training large birds."

Pepper rang his string of bells. "Come again! Come again!"

Examining his injured finger, Stuart winced. "A book sounds like a good idea."

Chase had a bad feeling about selling Pepper to this guy. He seemed to know nothing about parrots. Pepper didn't appear to like him, although his wife might be a different story. So was it even ethical to sell Stuart Peckam a bird?

"Will you take a credit card?" Stuart asked.

Six hundred dollars was a lot to turn down. Stuart had been the only nibble he'd gotten on Pepper

If he didn't sell Pepper now, he might never have another chance.

Would that really be such a bad thing? he wondered.

His palms began to sweat.

Stuart handed him the credit card.

Pepper hid his head under his wing as though saying, *Don't do it!*

Straightening his shoulders, Chase took the card. *Sorry, big guy. This is strictly business.*

Then why did it seem so wrong?

By the time he had packed up Pepper in his cage, and sold Stuart a bird book and some parrot food, Chase was feeling sick to his stomach. No matter how much he told himself the reason he'd accepted the bird from the guy whose mother had died was to sell it, the knot kept tightening in his belly.

"Thanks a lot for your help." Stuart tucked the book and food under one arm, and hefted the cage. "My wife is going to love Pepper."

Although Pepper was silent as the man carried him to his car, Chase's conscience spoke loudly.

Traitor! How could you sell Pepper? You love him. And he loves you.

Grabbing the charge slip he'd just filled out, Chase burst out the door onto the sidewalk. "Wait!" He hurried after Stuart, who had already reached his car. "I've changed my mind. I can't sell Pepper to you."

Stuart opened the back door of his car and put Pepper's cage inside. "What are you talking about? I just paid you six hundred bucks."

"I know. But he's worth way more than that." Chase darted around Stuart like a running back dodging a tackler. He grabbed Pepper's cage and stepped away from the car. "I'm really sorry. I hadn't realized... Pepper's not for sale." *I love him!* The realization that he was capable of so much love—for a bird!—made he wonder if Viv was right. Had he been selling himself short all these years?

Surely if his love for a bird—and all of this animals—was that strong, he could love Viv...and Theo...fully as much.

Stuart's expression darkened. "Are you crazy?"

"I was crazy to sell him. Here's your charge slip."

"I bought that bird fair and square." Instead of taking the credit slip, Stuart lunged for the birdcage.

"Help me! Help me!" Pepper squawked as Chase swung the cage out of Stuart's reach.

Patrick Fogerty, owner of The Fixer-Upper, came out of his shop next door. "Is there a problem?"

"This guy!" Stuart pointed an accusing finger at Chase. "He sold me that parrot. I'm giving it to my wife for her birthday. Now he's trying to take it back."

Patrick, at well over six feet, was an imposing

man and easily intimidating when he wanted to be. "Chase? What's going on?"

"I changed my mind. I can't sell Pepper." Chase knew he'd been slow on the uptake, but he'd realized *you can't sell or give away...something you love.* No price was high enough to make up for the loss.

Like the loss Viv would experience if she had to relinquish Theo.

Or the pain Chase would feel if he never had the chance to tell Viv how much he cared for her.

"Did you give him his money back?"

Chase held up the credit slip. "He can tear it up. I don't want his money."

Getting between Chase and his customer, Patrick took the credit slip and offered it to the man. "The bird stays here."

Stuart blustered, but Patrick stood his ground. So did Chase.

After a loud argument, Stuart drove away in an angry huff, promising never to shop in Bygones again.

When the car was out of sight, Patrick turned to Chase. "You sure that bird was worth losing a customer?"

Exhaling, Chase nodded. "Yeah, I do."

"Good birdie! Good birdie!" Pepper cooed.

By Wednesday, Vivian was a nervous wreck and Theo was teething, which meant she could barely put him down for a second without him starting to fuss.

This wasn't the part of mothering she had fantasized about for so many years. Even so, she wouldn't have missed a single minute for fear it would be the last one she would share with her baby boy.

Despite the bookstore being busy, Vivian had been so useless; Allison had wished her a happy Thanksgiving and sent her home early.

Of course, Theo stopped his fussing the moment she put him in the car and went immediately to sleep. *Poor tired little babykins.* She was tempted to keep driving around, so he'd get a proper nap. Except she'd been awake half the night and would probably fall asleep at the wheel herself.

How she wished she had someone to share the burden with, a shoulder to cry on when she felt down.

Someone like Chase.

But by choosing to adopt Theo, or at least trying her very best to adopt him, she'd given up all chance of being with Chase. And if she lost Theo? It wouldn't make any difference to Chase, because he knew she was determined to have a family of her own.

She blinked to clear her vision distorted by the tears she had refused to shed.

Once home, she gingerly carried Theo inside and

put him in his crib, praying he'd stay asleep long enough for her to check her blog for comments and read her email.

Allison had kindly taken out an advertisement on Vivian's blog that linked to Happy Endings, but so far she'd been unable to entice any other bookstore or regional business to advertise with her. She told herself it was early yet. Soon she'd attract more interest and followers, bringing advertisers to her site.

She eyed the pile of books sent to her for review by small publishers. If she didn't get more rest, she'd never be able to read them all.

With a sigh, she turned on her laptop. Three emails appeared. The first was from a high school friend; she'd deal with that later. The second was an announcement from the community playhouse in Manhattan, Kansas, about their upcoming Christmas musical. Too tired to think of even going out with friends to see the show, she deleted the email.

The third…

She stared at the third email, reading it slowly. From the marketing department of a small Midwestern travel company. They were inquiring about advertising rates on her blog. They felt readers of the books she reviewed might also be interested in guided tours of the heartland featuring historic and natural scenic sights.

Her heart stopped for a moment before kicking back into gear.

"Yes!" She pumped her fist in the air.

Within minutes, she had replied to the tour company, attaching her rate sheet as well as the purpose of her blog: to advance and call attention to heartland authors and their books.

A beginning! She felt it down deep in her being. She could and would make her blog a financial success. The Lord had shown her the way to achieve this goal. For that blessing she was grateful.

But whatever success she might achieve would be an empty one if Theo was taken from her.

Chapter Fifteen

On Thanksgiving, Vivian arrived at her parents' house a little before noon. Her car was packed with the assorted paraphernalia necessary to keep Theo happy for the day, plus two pies, one pumpkin and one pecan. Her mother was making a lemon meringue pie, a special favorite of Lisa's husband, Steve.

Lisa and her family had driven down from Chicago the day before, and their small SUV was parked between the house and the barn. Her twin brothers had already arrived, their full-size pickups parked cockeyed by the house.

The twins, along with Steve, Jake and Dad, were tossing a football around, warming up for their annual football game in the front yard. The two family dogs, Rufus and Betsy, were romping around trying to get into the game.

A perfect day for football; the sun was high in a

bright blue sky, and the temperature hinted at the coming of winter.

Pulling her car to a stop in the driveway, Vivian squeezed her eyes shut. Would Theo ever have a chance to play ball on Thanksgiving with his uncles?

All the men waved at her as she got out of the car, and she returned the greeting. Being with her family was a happy occasion, and she wasn't going to put a damper on the party.

The moment she stepped inside the front door, three-year-old Gracie came running toward her. "The baby! You bringed the baby!" She held up her arms for Theo.

"Hi, Gracie Sue." Vivian bent so Gracie could see the baby. "His name is Theo."

"He's a boy baby," Gracie announced.

"Yes, he is."

Vivian's mother came out from the kitchen. Her eyes were troubled as she greeted Vivian.

"There you are, dear." She gave Vivian a kiss on the cheek. "How are you?"

"All right, I guess. Terrified that any minute my phone is going to ring, and it will be Jackie with bad news."

"Well, not on Thanksgiving, I'm sure."

Gracie jumped up and down. "Can I hold the baby? Please? Please?"

"Mom, if you could supervise Gracie, I'll pu

Theo down on a blanket on the floor and go get the rest of the things from the car."

"Of course, dear."

Vivian passed Theo to her mother.

"Come on, Gracie. You and Grandma are going to get acquainted with Theo."

Comfortable she was leaving Theo in good hands, Vivian went out to her car.

"Hey there, Vivi." Her sister Lisa came running out after her. Slightly taller than Vivian, Lisa had their father's dark hair and their mother's quick smile.

They hugged, Lisa holding her a moment longer than usual.

"Mom told me you might lose Theo. I'm so sorry."

"Yeah, so am I. But it hasn't happened yet, so for today I'm not going to worry about it." She quickly crossed her fingers and hoped she didn't have cause to worry.

"That's my brave little sis." She hugged her again. "Let me help you carry stuff in. I remember how it takes a pack mule to haul everything you need for a baby."

Vivian laughed, the first good laugh she'd had in some time. It felt so good to see her sister. They'd been close growing up, and Vivian missed her every day. A couple of phone calls a month and checking in with each other on Facebook didn't seem like enough.

With their arms full, they walked up onto the porch.

"Mom tells me you might have a gentleman friend coming to dinner today," Lisa said.

Vivian halted. A wave of sadness washed over her. "I don't know if he's coming or not. Mom asked me to invite anyone who might not have a place to go for Thanksgiving dinner. But he hasn't said anything lately." Nor had she reminded him. She'd been too wrapped up in the possibility of losing Theo and too upset that Chase didn't understand how that was tearing her apart.

"Well, I, for one, think he'd be a fool not to show up. Mom's making enough food for an army, as usual, and every bit of it is going to taste delicious. Besides, if he's got good sense, he shouldn't let someone like you get away."

Vivian wasn't quite sure how she felt about Chase now. She wanted him to come to dinner, sure. But she wanted so much more from him. Things that he didn't seem able to give.

Chase took Boyo for a walk Thanksgiving morning. They strolled over to Bronson Park, where they watched kids playing and dads tossing balls to their children. Parents and their children all seemed to be having fun.

Families.

That made Chase think of Viv. She was probably at her parents' house by now, there with her brothers and sisters. And Theo, assuming the adoption agency hadn't snatched him away from her yet.

How would she ever survive losing Theo?

It had been hard enough on Chase when he had almost sold Pepper. And Pepper was only a bird. How much worse would it be for Viv to lose the baby she'd grown to love?

Back at Fluff & Stuff, he checked his watch.

According to Viv, her mother had invited him to Thanksgiving dinner. It was probably going to be a good one. Lots better than eating at the Red Rooster.

But would Viv want him there?

He hadn't understood what she was going through. He hadn't gotten that a woman like Viv could give her heart to a baby so quickly.

Of course, Theo was pretty cute. He'd sort of grown on Chase, too.

He went to the front window and looked out. Main Street was as quiet as he'd ever seen it. A lonely place for someone without a family.

"What do you think, Pepper?" he asked. "Do you think the Duncans' invitation still holds? Or that Viv wouldn't want me within ten feet of her?"

"Good birdie! Good birdie!" Pepper crooned.

Boyo barked at Chase as though agreeing with Pepper. Boyo sat, gazing up with soulful brown eyes.

Maybe he could get back into Viv's good graces if he let her know he was finally beginning to understand. If she did have to give up Theo, Chase should be around to console her.

But he couldn't show up at the Duncan house for dinner with empty hands. All the stores in Bygones were closed. The owners were no doubt enjoying their own Thanksgiving celebrations.

Trying to come up with an idea that would work, he walked to the back of the shop to check on the puppies in the pen. They tumbled around, yipping at each other.

He could have taken Mrs. Duncan some flowers if he'd planned ahead. But Love in Bloom was closed tight. Lily and Tate Bronson wouldn't appreciate his interrupting their first Thanksgiving as a married couple.

Then he remembered the field of sunflowers he'd driven past when he and Viv were going to visit Happy Havens Animal Shelter. He smiled to himself.

A big bouquet of sunflowers might just do the trick.

"Viv, honey, do you think we ought to go ahead and serve?" her mother asked. "Or do you want to wait a while?"

The smell of roasted turkey, rich gravy laced with giblets and baked yam casserole with marshmallows filled the overheated kitchen.

Vivian checked her watch. Three o'clock on the button. Her shoulders slumped. Chase wasn't coming to dinner. Despite knowing he wasn't likely to show, disappointment raked through her spirit. She had been so hopeful he'd be able to see and understand how upset she'd been about Theo.

Apparently not only didn't he want to be a father, he didn't want to deal with a woman's emotional ups and downs.

"I think we ought to go ahead," Vivian said, resigned to the fact Chase wasn't coming. "Let's call the guys in, and we'll get started. If he was going to come, I think he would have been here by now."

Lisa gave her a hug. "Sorry, sis. Men. You can't live with 'em, and you can't live without 'em."

"I don't appear to have a choice except to live without them." Vivian picked up a hot pad and carried the yam casserole into the dining room.

Sophie was right behind her with the bowl of string beans and a dish of cranberry sauce. "Personally, I don't plan to ever marry. The boys I know aren't worth the effort."

Smiling wistfully, Vivian remembered having the same feeling when she was in high school. An attitude she'd outgrown by the time she had turned twenty. Not that the change in attitude had done her much good.

From the back bedroom where Theo was napping, she heard his cry. "So much for a quiet dinner. Theo's awake." She handed the hot pad to Sophie and went to get her son. Vivian had hoped he would sleep through dinner, but it seemed right that he'd be up and awake for his first Thanksgiving dinner with the Duncan family.

But please not the last.

By the time she changed Theo and got back to the dining room, the food was on the table and everyone was standing around waiting for her.

"Sorry," she said. She slipped Theo into his high chair next to her place and propped pillows around him so he wouldn't slip out. "Everything looks wonderful, Mom."

David, the older of her twin brothers by about two minutes, held out her chair for her while Daniel held their mother's. For some reason, the place that had been set for Chase hadn't been removed. It was an unpleasant reminder that he hadn't even thought to call to decline her mother's invitation.

Vivian was about to sit when the doorbell chimed.

Her gaze flew toward the front door, and her breath snagged in her throat.

"I'll get it," her dad said.

When Gene opened the door, Chase stepped in

side. Dressed in slacks and a nice sport shirt, he was carrying a huge bouquet of sunflowers.

"Oh, my…" Vivian touched her chest where her heart was thundering against her rib cage.

"Sorry I'm late." Chase took in the family at the dining table, his eyes searching out Vivian. His wary expression suggested he didn't know if he'd be welcomed.

A tentative smile lifting her lips, Vivian touched the vacant chair beside her. "We saved a place for you." There was a place in her heart for him, too, if only he were willing to accept it.

"Here, let me take those gorgeous flowers from you." Her mother hurried to greet Chase. "It will just take me a minute to find a vase, and then we can eat. Do sit down, Chase. We're so glad you came."

While her mother took care of the flowers, Vivian made the introductions. David and Daniel eyed Chase with a bit of overly protective brotherly love, but they were at least polite.

Lisa was far more effervescent. "We were all hopeful you'd make it to dinner. Viv hasn't told me hardly a thing about you, so I will be plying you with dozens of questions. I hope you don't mind."

"Lisa!" Vivian admonished her sister, who simply grinned in return.

Chase flushed. "From the looks of things, if that's

the price of having one of your mother's home-cooked dinners, I think I can handle a few questions."

"Perfect answer," Vivian whispered.

He gave her a sly smile. "I try. Sometimes it takes me a while to get it right."

Her mother returned with a tall vase filled with sunflowers. "This is so special. Thank you, Chase."

"You're more than welcome."

Under her breath, Vivian asked, "I thought Love in Bloom was closed today. Did you have to drag Lily back to the shop?"

"Nope. I picked those myself, which is part of the reason I'm late. I hadn't planned ahead, but I remembered seeing them on the road the time we drove out to Happy Havens together."

It took her a moment to recall the flowers, then she took his hand and squeezed it. "They're perfect. I can't imagine a better gift for Mother. Both she and Dad are Kansas natives."

"They're for you, too. I wanted a way to say I'm sorry for not understanding what you were going through about Theo."

Sudden tears burned at the back of her eyes. Her fears and insecurities melted away, replaced by a reignited spark of hope.

As soon as her mother was seated, followed by everyone else, her father gave a short prayer of grace. The dishes began circling the table, and conversation began to flow.

To the twins' dismay, it turned out Chase was a Kansas City Chiefs fan when everyone at the table rooted for the Atlanta Falcons.

Ignoring the gibes, Chase changed the subject. "I could sure use another slice of white meat and some gravy."

"There's always plenty more," her mother said, and the dishes were passed around to him.

He nudged Vivian. "Is there salt on the table?"

"Oh, sure." She stretched to the middle of the table to reach the pair of ceramic salt-and-pepper shakers that looked like miniature pilgrims.

Chase examined the salt shaker. "Cute."

She smiled at the memory they represented. "I bought those at the dollar store in town when I was about ten and gave them to my mother for her birthday. She's had them on the Thanksgiving table ever since."

"Nice."

Their eyes met, and something warm and wonderful passed between them that had Vivian forgetting she was surrounded by her family. For a moment, Chase was the only other person in the room.

Amid all the talking and laughter, Theo began to fuss. Rattles and bites of mushy rice didn't seem to appease him, so Vivian decided she'd have to give him a bottle. She went to the kitchen and returned to settle the baby in her arms.

"You've been taking care of Theo so much, you've hardly had a chance to eat," Chase pointed out. "Why don't you let me feed him?"

Her mouth opened, and she gaped at him. "You're sure?"

"How hard can it be?" He slid his chair back and held up his hands for the baby.

Not entirely confident he knew what he was doing, she handed Theo to Chase along with the baby's bottle.

He cuddled Theo in the crook of his arm. "Hey, big guy. We've got to give your mom a break, huh? She needs to eat, too." Awkwardly, he managed to get the nipple in Theo's mouth. The baby did the rest, never taking his eyes off Chase as he drained the bottle.

Vivian couldn't recall seeing anything more beautiful, any man who was more tender and caring, than Chase, feeding the baby she loved. She'd been so emotional since the phone call about the possibility of losing Theo, the sight of the two of them so engaged with each other nearly undid her.

Please, Lord, let my dreams come true.

After dinner, while the women cleaned up the kitchen, Chase found himself on the floor with Theo and three-year-old Gracie. The child had insisted he play tea party with her and the baby.

The TV was playing. The men were all sitting

around trying to digest the huge meal they'd eaten. From the kitchen, the chatter of women at work drifted out. A phone buzzed somewhere.

Suddenly the women's conversation halted. Chase looked up and saw Viv walking hurriedly toward the back bedrooms with a phone at her ear.

The hairs on his nape rose. His stomach clenched, and he got a flash of déjà vu.

He pushed himself to his feet. "Guys, can one of you supervise the tea party for me? I've got to see—" He left the thought unfinished as he followed after Viv. He didn't want to butt in. The call could be from anybody and none of his business. So he lingered in the hallway. Listening. Waiting. In case Viv needed him.

"Yes, I understand." Her voice sounded shaky.

Absently, Chase ran his finger across the scar on his chin. *Please don't let her lose Theo.*

"That…soon?" She choked on the word.

After a moment, she whispered, "Thank you."

Chase couldn't stand it any longer. He stepped into the bedroom. Tears were streaming down Viv's face, and she was gulping air as though she couldn't catch her breath.

"Aw, sweetheart. I'm so sorry." He took her into his arms. "We'll fight this together. Somehow we'll figure out a way that you can keep Theo. You're the best mother he could ever have. I won't let them take him away from you."

She shook her head. "I'm not…crying because of that." She hiccupped. "That phone call was *good* news." Her lips quivered into a smile. "I get to keep Theo!"

"That's…that's terrific!"

She started to sob even harder. "But if I keep Theo, I'm going to lose you," she wailed. "I don't want to—"

"Shh, it's all right." He held her tight, stroking her soft, silky hair. "You aren't going to lose me. I'm staying right here with you."

She lifted her head. "You are?"

He swallowed hard and licked his lips. Even if he didn't deserve Viv, losing her would be worse that selling Pepper. He loved that silly parrot. But what he felt for Viv was ten times, a thousand times more powerful than any emotion he'd ever experienced.

He caressed her cheek. "I've been so totally stupid and dense. Please forgive me."

"There's nothing to forgive you for."

"Yeah, there is. I want to take care of you. And Theo. I'm not much of a catch. And I'm still scared of being a father. But I want to make it work. I want you to help me be the best, most loving dad that Theo could ever have."

"Oh, Chase…" She looked up at him with watery eyes and palmed his cheek. "I'm sorry for what happened to you as a boy. But I've seen you with Theo. And Sam's twins and little Gracie. You're going to be a wonderful father. I know you are. But if you want to wait until you're sure—"

"I've never been more sure of anything in my life. I love you, Vivian Duncan. I love Theo, too. I didn't realize what you were going through, but now I do." Almost losing Pepper had awakened him to what love was all about. Granted it was odd that a silly parrot had taught him about love. But that's what happened. He wasn't going to lose someone he loved, if he could help it. That meant doing all he could to not lose Viv.

"I love you, too. I think I have since you sold me the hamster." She laughed, a happy sound that lifted Chase's heart.

"Then you'll marry me?"

"Marry? Aren't we moving a little fast here?"

"I'm not going to risk losing you, Viv. Say you'll marry me, please."

"Yes! A thousand times, yes!" More watery tears began to fall despite the smile that blossomed, making her look more beautiful than ever.

He framed her face with his hands and kissed her deeply, trying to communicate with all of his heart how very much he loved her.

Someone knocked on the open bedroom door and cleared her throat.

They both looked up.

"Sorry to bother you," her mother said, her gaze

sliding from Viv to Chase and back again. "I was wondering if everything was all right."

"Mom, everything is wonderful. Chase and Theo and I are getting married! We're going to be a family."

Vivian didn't think she'd ever been hugged and kissed so many times. Chase must have felt like he was being initiated into some backslapping, hand-shaking, cheek-kissing fraternity.

After more than an hour, she and Chase finally had a chance to slip out onto the porch to be alone for a few minutes. With Theo sound asleep in the back bedroom, Chase led her to a shadowed part of the porch and kissed her deeply. Her whole body responded as though it recognized this wonderful, sweet man she loved. She held on to his broad shoulders as he pulled her closer. His masculine scent and the taste of his lips on hers were a heady combination that sent her head reeling.

When he finally broke the kiss, she was breathing heavily.

"That's quite a welcome to the family I got," he said, wrapping his arms around her again to keep her warm against the cold night air.

"They love you already."

"I thought I heard a couple of threats about what would happen to me if I wasn't good to you. Definitely put me on my best behavior."

She laughed. "They're all harmless, I promise."

"I hope so. Those twins are pretty formidable when they're together." He stroked her face, his hand warm against her cheek. "I want to get you a ring, Viv."

"You don't have to do that."

"Yeah, I do. I want everyone to know you're mine, and that I love you. You can have as long an engagement as you need to be sure this will be right for you. But I want you to go with me to Wichita to pick out something you like." Her heart was so full, she could barely contain it within her chest. "I'd love to go shopping with you."

"I can't go tomorrow. I'm expecting a big day at the shop, and Maureen starts work tomorrow morning."

"Oh, that's right. I'm so glad you hired her. I'm sure she'll be a hard worker."

"Do you think Allison will give you Saturday off to go to Wichita?"

She chuckled and kissed him on his cheek. "If I tell Allison why I need the day off, she'll probably throw me out the door. She's quite a romantic at heart."

"There sure has been a lot of romance going on in Bygones since all the new shops opened up."

"And ours is the best romance of all."

Epilogue

Monday morning, Coraline came flying into Happy Endings. She headed directly for Vivian, who was shelving a new shipment of books in the mystery section.

"Rumors have been flying all around town," Coraline announced.

"About what? Who the town benefactor is?"

"Well, that, too. But I was referring to a certain young lady who is now engaged to be married."

As was typical, Vivian felt heat rush to her cheeks. "I plead guilty." She held out her hand to show Coraline her engagement ring. Together she and Chase had picked out a ring with a traditional round-cut solitaire diamond in the center and a smaller diamond on each side.

"Lovely! It looks absolutely perfect on you. Your hands are so delicate and pretty." She squeezed Vivian's hand.

"It's set in white gold. I liked that better than the yellow gold."

Coraline gave her a hug. "I'm so happy for you. Chase is a good man, and he is blessed to land you for his wife."

"We don't want to rush things, though. We're thinking we might marry sometime next spring. Maybe in May."

"It's a good idea to take your time," Coraline agreed. "You'll both have many happy years together."

Vivian placed her hand over her racing heart. "I feel so blessed that Chase loves me, and I love him so much," Vivian said. "And he's going to be a fabulous father for Theo. He had us stop at a toy store, and he bought Theo a tiny soft football. He said it wasn't too early to start his training."

Laughing, Coraline shook her head. "Isn't that just like a man?"

"I'm not too sure about Theo playing football, so I countered by buying a picture book about animals. He may want to follow in Chase's footsteps and take over Fluff & Stuff when he grows up."

Allison appeared from the back room. "It would be wonderful if all the SOS shop owners would have children who wanted to stay right here in Bygones and keep growing our community."

"That would be fantastic," Coraline agreed.

"We'll need lots of children if we want to keep the school going."

"Speaking of children," Allison said, "tell Coraline about the idea you and Chase came up with to help at-risk students."

"Well, it's just an idea so far." Vivian set aside the book she was holding. "Chase and I were talking over dinner last night, and Rory Liston's name came up, and the trouble he's in. We thought there ought to be some way to help young people who are having trouble at home or school."

"At-risk children," Coraline provided.

"Yes, that's what we meant. Anyway, that led to us thinking about how young children learn to be responsible by taking care of animals, either by helping with the family pets or through 4-H programs."

"That's true," Allison agreed. "But I don't understand how that would help someone like Rory."

"Chase thought if there was a way to match a youngster to one of the dogs at the shelter, put him in charge of feeding and bathing and walking the animal, it would be good for both the youngster and the shelter animals."

"Why, yes!" Coraline brought her hands together as though in prayer. "I've been trying to come up with something and that sounds perfect."

Vivian beamed. "It will take some organizing."

"Chief Sheridan ought to be brought in on the

idea," Allison suggested. "That kind of program could be an alternative to putting a teenager in jail for something like Rory did. More like community service."

"If we knew who the town benefactor was, maybe we could talk him, or her, into funding a social worker to work out of the school, identifying at-risk students," Vivian suggested.

Coraline's eyes widened at the possibility. "What a wonderful idea. *If* we knew who the benefactor was."

Vivian's forehead tightened into a frown, and she recalled seeing Coraline and Robert Randall in deep conversation at the church Thanksgiving dinner. "Do you know who he is?" she asked.

"You mean he or she, don't you?" Coraline countered.

"Well, do you?" Vivian asked, seeing a spark in Coraline's eyes that raised Vivian's excitement about discovering the identity of the benefactor.

"Now, now. If I did know—and I'm not saying I do—don't you think we ought to wait until he or she reveals that secret in his or her own good time?"

"No!" Vivian and Allison chorused, and then they laughed.

"If you know who it is, you have to tell us," Vivian pleaded.

Allison echoed the feeling. "Really, we've all

been going crazy trying to figure out who it is. Please tell us."

Coraline looked up at the ceiling as though the answer might be written there. She pondered their request for a long moment, which put Vivian's nerves on edge.

"Coraline?" she questioned.

"I think, my dears, that waiting is good for the soul. But I imagine that all will be revealed soon." She smiled serenely and backed toward the door. "Quite soon."

* * * * *

Dear Reader,

My younger daughter has always been an animal lover. In fact, her first job at age sixteen was at a pet store. Knowing that made it fun to create Fluff & Stuff and get to know the new owner, Chase Rollings. Watching him struggle with his past and grow into a man who learns the meaning of love was a journey worth traveling. In my view, Chase had to be strong to match the inner strength of Vivian Duncan. She is the kind of woman who takes control of her own life without giving up a bit of her generous, loving heart. They seem a perfect match to me.

I confess I've never lived in a small town like Bygones, Kansas. I live in a suburb of Los Angeles. But the truth is, my hometown is something of a small town, too. I meet friends at the grocery store and know the clerks and manager; I've personally known our mayors and city council members. While there may be many strangers who live in this town, I feel comforted by my friendships. I hope you feel that way about your hometown, too, no matter how large or small.

Working with the other authors of the Heart of Main Street continuity has been a treat. Arlene James, Carolyne Aarsen, Brenda Minton, Lissa Manley and Valerie Hansen have shared their

stories, characters and creativity, making the wor
easier for everyone. I thank them and look forwar
to meeting them in person and working with ther
again.

You, the reader, bring something to this story, a
well: your past experiences and your dreams of th
future. Without you, the story would lack essentia
ingredients. Thank you for being a part of the tale

Charlotte Carter

Questions for Discussion

1. In this story, Chase was afraid he would become like his abusive father. Is that a reasonable fear?

2. Do you know any small towns like Bygones, Kansas, that have suffered economically and then become reinvigorated with an influx of new businesses? How did they manage that?

3. Have you ever had a parrot as a pet? How do they differ from owning a dog or cat? If you don't have a parrot, would you want one?

4. Where do you buy most of your books? At an independent bookstore like Happy Endings? A chain store? Online? Why?

5. What sort of pets do you have in your household? What do you gain by owning pets?

6. Have you ever worked at a pet store? Do you think you would enjoy that experience?

7. If you were unable to have children, would you adopt a child? Why or why not?

8. Do you have any special-needs children in your family? What has your experience been watching them grow up?

9. What do you remember most about four-month-old babies?

10. Does your church have a special program to help the less fortunate during the holidays? Describe what your church does.

11. What special dishes do you serve at Thanksgiving that others may not?

12. Have you ever adopted an animal from a shelter? What was your experience like?

13. Are you a regular volunteer at an animal shelter, hospital or other nonprofit organization? What do you get out of volunteering?

14. Is there an antigraffiti program in your town? Is it effective?

15. Do you read blogs written by authors or visit their websites? Are you active on social media sites such as Facebook and Twitter? Why or why not?

LARGER-PRINT BOOKS!

GET 2 FREE
LARGER-PRINT NOVELS
PLUS 2 FREE
MYSTERY GIFTS

Love Inspired

Larger-print novels are now available...

Reader Service.com

Manage your account online!
- Review your order history
- Manage your payments
- Update your address

*We've designed
the Harlequin® Reader Service
website just for you.*

Enjoy all the features!
- Reader excerpts from any series
- Respond to mailings and special monthly offers
- Discover new series available to you
- Browse the Bonus Bucks catalog
- Share your feedback